THE BOOT OF DESTINY

BOOKS BY CLARK

THE STAINS OF TIME

The Piano of Death

The Boot of Destiny

The Chains of Desire

The Elixir of Denial

The Dance of Dreams

OTHER BOOKS

Those Little Bastards

All He Left Behind

Missing Mr. Wingfield

The Seven Wives of Silver

Bad Poetry Night

Out of the Woods

Under the World

THE BOOT OF DESTINY

E. CHRISTOPHER CLARK

Published in the United States by Clarkwoods in Chelmsford, Massachusetts.

ISBN for the Print Edition: 978-1-952044-12-0
ISBN for the Digital Edition: 978-1-952044-13-7

Library of Congress Control Number: 2020902233

For my kids

I

THE BASTARD SONS OF BASTARDS

NOVEMBER 2010

When Tracy was called to the principal's office to answer for the pantsing of Brian Meltzer, the first question that Old Lady Standish asked was, "Is he the first boy to break your heart?"

"Oh no," said Tracy.

"There was someone else?"

"Yes," she said. "A telephone man who fell in love with long distances."

"A what kind of a man?"

"Mr. Wingfield," said Tracy, plucking one pencil from Standish's Reese's Peanut Butter mug, then another.

On the other side of the desk, the principal moved her computer's mouse around. Then, once she'd gotten her cursor to wherever it was she wanted it to go, she began to hunt and peck at her keyboard. "Wingfield, you said?"

Tracy rolled her eyes, lining up pencils on the desk, their dull points aimed at the dull old woman. "Have you ever seen *The Glass Menagerie?*" she asked.

"Is that Wilde or Williams?" asked the principal, still typing away with her index fingers. "I always get them mixed up."

"Well, they do both begin with a W," said Tracy, trying to hide her incredulity, but forgetting to mask her sarcasm in the process.

Principal Standish stopped typing, folded her hands in front of her, and stared over the glasses that sat precipitously on the edge of her nose. She was stone-faced for a moment, then two, but soon enough a smirk cracked through the veneer and she shook her head. Then she pushed her seat back from the desk, rose, and crossed to her bookshelf. She plucked a dusty old Norton anthology from the top shelf and returned to her seat.

"The pages are so thin," said Tracy, as she watched the old woman leaf through the tome.

"Just a smidge thicker than tissue paper," said Standish, "but there's a whole lot of canon to cram between two covers. Anything heavier and—"

Standish went silent, adjusted her spectacles, and read. She moved her lips for the first few words, then caught herself.

Though she would never say so out loud, Tracy was thankful that Principal Standish didn't consider her God's gift to Harwich High School. From the moment she'd transferred here, all those years ago, everyone else had treated her like some kind of golden child. How miraculous she was for having survived the divorce of her parents, the marriage of her mother to another woman. How astounding that, despite all the trouble in her life, she'd not only survived, but thrived. Tracy remembered the first spelling test she'd taken here on the Cape, back in the third grade, how the teacher had applauded the emotionally bruised child for spelling *knight* correctly on her first try. How hard it must be to string six letters together—some of them silent!—when your soul was as black and blue as hers. Tracy could still feel that teacher's hands on her shoulders, the sympathetic squeeze. She could still feel the fire in her cheeks as she tried not to look any of her new class-mates in the eye.

"Which Mr. Wingfield?" Standish asked. "The son or the father?"

Tracy smirked, then thought better of it and ducked her head. Damned pompousness coming out again.

"The father," said Standish, closing the book, its two halves slapping together in her arthritic hand.

"Most people forget he's there," said Tracy.

"But he isn't," said Standish. "And that's the point."

On one of his visits home from Hawaii a few years before, Tracy's Uncle Michael had taken her into Cambridge to see a play one of his college housemates was putting on at some derelict building just outside the ivy-covered walls of Harvard. It wasn't a theater, this place; it was more like an old house. But that was perfect, Uncle Michael told her, "exactly what this guy's been imagining since the first time he read the script."

The script, of course, was *The Glass Menagerie*, and Tracy traced the abstract lines on its cover—the dog and the giraffe and all the rest—as Michael covered his ears on the Green Line, the ceaseless whine of the subway car driving him batty.

While they changed trains at Park Street, Michael, rubbing at his temples, told her about the thing he was most looking forward to. "The photo of the father," he said.

"The father?" Tracy asked him. "What father?"

Michael laughed. "Everyone forgets about the father, but my pal, the director, he wrote his whole thesis on the dude."

"But he's not in the play, Uncle Michael. The father isn't around."

"Yeah," said Michael. "And that's why he's so important."

Tracy recalled little of the forgettable production, but she would never forget the comically large portrait of the smiling soldier in the doughboy's cap, his toothy grin frozen in sepia forever. It hung above the mantle of the working fireplace, which roared throughout the show, and it was so big that the stage lights actually obscured the top of his head, his hat.

"On purpose," Michael had told her. "All on purpose."

Maybe, Tracy had thought, but she realized even then, even as young as she was, that a decision made on purpose could be a bad decision just the same.

"Do you miss your father?" Standish asked.

"I thought we were here to talk about me pantsing Brian," said Tracy, picking pencils up off the desk and replacing them in the cup.

"We are," said Standish.

"Okay," said Tracy. "Good."

Brian Meltzer was a schmuck, the kind of kid who helped a hot girl with her homework then stared at her ass as she walked away, a smug grin on his face, like he'd earned the ogle. They all went to him when they came to the tutoring center, though. It wasn't that they minded Tracy; it's just that she wouldn't do their work for them. And she'd tried to tell them, for the past four years, what kind of a kid Brian was, but they didn't care. "Do you know how you're paying for all that extra help?" she'd ask.

"It's just our asses," they'd say. "And he's not the only one. And at least we're getting something out of it with him."

Tracy would sigh, they'd wave a dismissive hand, and that would be the end of it.

"What made this morning different?" asked Standish. "What pushed you over the edge?"

"I'm mad as hell," said Tracy, "and I'm not going to take it anymore."

Standish laughed. "A great film, that one. Have you seen it, or just caught clips on YouTube?"

"Unlike the men in my family, I—"

"I thought we weren't talking about your family," said Standish, an eyebrow raised.

"Touché," said Tracy.

Standish smirked, gave a curt nod, and directed her attention to her window. Tracy looked now, too. School buses were lining up in a neat row outside. The doors to two of them opened and the drivers, one male and one female, stepped out. They chatted amiably, the woman offering the man a stick of gum.

"Years ago," said Standish, "they would have been smoking."

"Nasty habit," said Tracy. "Killed my great-grandfather."

"Do you know what kind of chemicals they put in chewing gum, Ms. Silver? Or in those Diet Cokes you guzzle like they're going out of style?"

She knows what I drink at lunch? thought Tracy.

Standish pulled a manila folder from a wire rack stuffed with them and plucked a form from it, one of those horrible triplicate things, the yellow form bound for home, the pink for the teacher who filed the complaint, the white for Tracy's permanent record.

As Standish began to write, Tracy gave an *ahem*.

"Yes."

"Just so it's clear, I had no idea Brian was going commando today."

"Commando?" said Standish.

"Commando," said Tracy. "You know: sans underpants."

Standish grinned, shook her head. "I've never heard that term."

"My mothers let me watch too many *Friends* reruns as a kid."

Standish finished writing, then handed the form over to Tracy to read.

"The surprise appearance of Mr. Meltzer's penis did not factor into your punishment," she said.

Tracy nodded, took the lone pen from the Reese's cup—you couldn't sign these things in pencil, right?—and signed. "One day's suspension seems fair," she said. "And it gives me extra time to pack for my college visit this weekend."

"I've forgotten," said Standish. "Where are you headed?"

"Hawaii," said Tracy. "To visit my uncle and check out U of H. He teaches there," she added. "Illustration and art history."

Standish nodded. "Maybe take the play with you," she said, "and re-read it on the flight."

"You think I missed something?" said Tracy.

Standish bit her thumb and considered Tracy for a moment.

"I did," said Tracy, "didn't I?"

"Are you aware of Mr. Meltzer's home situation, Ms. Silver?"

Tracy nodded. "Lives with his mom," she said, "which, if I can say, makes his behavior even more—"

Standish raised a finger and Tracy shut herself up.

"It's not just the Lauras of the world who are missing their old men," said Standish. "It's the Toms, too."

Tracy nodded again, tore off the bottom copy of the form, and then folded it into a square. She stuffed that into the front pocket of her jeans.

Standish said, "We'll see you in a couple of days then."

Tracy nodded one last time, but the gesture felt all wrong. There were words left to be said, and she had not yet mastered the art of holding her tongue. She envisioned this for a second, actually pinching the fleshy instrument of her self-destruction between thumb and forefinger, and the pause was just long enough for Standish to notice.

"Yes?" said Standish.

Tracy ducked her head and half-mumbled, "Permission to speak freely?"

"Permission to what?" said Standish.

Tracy looked up. "Don't you think your reading of the text is a little heteronormative?"

Standish raised an eyebrow.

"I mean, Laura and Tom's issues with their mother have more to do with Amanda's psychoses than the lack of a father figure. Amanda would be messed up even if her husband were still there." Tracy paused, bit her lip, tried to hold back. But she couldn't. "Not every work in the canon is centered around daddy issues," she said. "My life isn't any worse because I have two mothers, Mrs. Standish. It just isn't."

"Ms. Silver," said Standish, steepling her hands in front of her face for a moment, then unsteepling them, then smiling the smile of a woman who's just dropped a deuce in her pantsuit. "You will undoubtedly be the valedictorian of your class. Your performance here, occasional lapses in judgment notwithstanding, is so far beyond the standards we have set that our faculty struggles to challenge you. My point: you could attend any college you wanted, and I know you have been courted by a great many of them."

"Yes," said Tracy. "And?"

"And yet," said Standish, "your first choice, if you'll permit *me* to speak freely, is a second- or third-tier school whose sole perk is its proximity to the only male authority figure you have ever truly valued."

Tracy felt her brow furrow, felt an eyebrow raise, felt words ready to tumble from her mouth. But once more, just as she was about to speak, Standish raised a solitary finger.

"Ms. Silver," Standish began again. "Your mothers are among the finest parents I've dealt with in all the many years I've been at this school. This has nothing to do with them and everything to do with you."

"I don't need a father," said Tracy.

Standish gave the briefest of chuckles. "It's funny," she said. "Mr. Meltzer said the same thing. And yet, when his father came to pick him up this morning, to take him away for the Thanksgiving holiday, his face was lighter than I've ever seen it. As for you, Ms. Silver, isn't it true that your college essay is about the rise and fall of your uncle's band?"

"Yes," said Tracy, "but—"

Old Lady Standish shushed her one last time. Then she stood, crossed to the door, and made ready to open it.

Tracy stood and stepped toward the door. But Standish still hadn't opened it. "A final lesson?" she asked.

"Consider this," said Standish, her hand fiddling with the knob, "I never said you were a Laura. Maybe," she said, "you're a Tom."

Tracy rolled her eyes and sighed, "I don't think you understand what I meant by heteronorma—"

Standish shook her head and finally pulled open the door. "Good afternoon, Ms. Silver," she said. "Have a safe flight."

"I have, like, so much more to say about this," said Tracy. "It is totally unfair the way teachers start a debate and then end it before—"

Standish set a hand on Tracy's shoulder and squeezed. Then she nudged her out of the office. "Oh," said Standish with a smile, "the maelstrom your mothers have set loose upon our unsuspecting world."

And, not knowing whether to take these words as a compliment, an insult, or something somewhere in between, Tracy watched Old Lady Standish shut the door.

❧ II ❧
WHAT TO LOOK FOR IN
A MAN
MARCH 2011

Once upon a time, they used the old barn as a garage and nothing more. But these days, the creaky old outbuilding was whatever they needed it to be. In the past year, it had been the office of a gesticulating attorney, the apartment of southern woman and her crippled daughter, the drawing room of an English manor, and, of course, an uninhabited island on which a Neapolitan ship had just wrecked. Tonight, this weekend, it was an approximation of the house that had once stood just up the hill, of that house's parlor in particular. And tonight, more than any other night—and that was saying something—it seemed haunted by the spirits the actors had conjured. All was quiet, and all were gone, but Tracy Silver did not feel alone.

She crept across the stage with a milk crate, tidying up. So many props in this one: there was an opened box on the coffee table, an overturned tea cup and saucer next to that, and a discarded apron beneath the ornate Victorian chair that sat center stage. Off to one corner rested a bloodied and muddied boot, the kind a mariner might wear—*the* boot her own ancestor had worn, it turned out. Tracy picked it up last, set her crate on the table, and then slumped down into the chair.

She held the boot the way she might hold Yorick's skull, if her mothers ever gave her the chance, and she looked upon it the way she imagined the Dane might look upon the final remains of that infinite jester: with puzzlement and melancholy and then, just at the end, with a hint of righteous anger.

Tracy slipped off her own shoe and made to fit the boot upon her foot, but she was stopped short. Just outside the theater, there were voices approaching, four of them. She dropped the boot and hurried toward the back of the stage, making for the alcove that led upstairs to the dressing rooms and the attic. But she did not flee to the upper levels, not yet. She hid behind the door and listened.

"What I've never understood," said Desiree, "is why your grandfather's sister—"

"—Great Aunt Dottie—" said Veronica, yawning.

"Yes," said Desiree. "The cartoonist! That's the one. I've never understood why she needed an alias in the first place."

There was another voice now, a man's, Michael's. He said, "Did you read my book?"

"I tried," said Desiree. "But, y'know, Professor Smarty-Pants, we needed something to replace the coffee table's broken leg and—"

There was laughter then, even from Michael, who went on to say something about lesbians breaking into comics in the 1940s. Tracy stopped listening, tried to tune him out. It was one thing to see him from across the way, as she had tonight,—and as she had, unbeknownst to him, on the night in Hawaii when he ruined everything—but it was another to hear him speak. She wasn't ready for that yet, not after what had happened. Soon—the nip bottle in the cooler out back had been prepared especially for this confrontation, after all—but not now. Tracy looked down at her feet as she tried to summon a song, something to drown him out, but before even one note had hummed its way through her brain, another damned thing grabbed her attention. Her right foot, it was bare. Her shoe was still on stage.

Without thinking, she raced back to grab it. And that, of course, was when they spotted her.

"Hey," said Michael. "There's the girl of the hour."

"Hi," said Tracy.

"Where are you off to?" said Michael.

Jenna nudged him with her elbow. "Can't you see she's striking the set?"

"There's not someone else who can do that?" said Michael.

Tracy knelt to put her shoe back on. "It's my job," she said as she tied her laces.

"Says who?" said Michael.

"Says Mum," said Tracy, pointing at Veronica, who had slumped into the chair, eyes closed.

"Veronica!" said Michael.

"Nnnwhat?"

"Did you tell Tracy she had to clean up this mess?"

"It's her job," said Veronica.

Michael turned to face Desiree. "C'mon, seriously, you let her saddle the kid with—"

"I'm just the stepmom," said Desiree. "Veronica gave birth to her. She makes the rules."

Tracy stood, brushing dust off the knee of her stage blacks. "We run a theater out of our barn," she said. "Everyone has to do their part, Michael. It's fine."

"It's not fine," he said. "You've been busy over here since the moment Jenna and I got to town. I haven't even had a second to congratulate you on—Hey, wait, did you just call me Michael?"

Jenna chuckled. "That is your name, dear."

"No," said Michael. "I know. But... what happened to the Uncle part?"

"Technically," said Tracy, "you're not my uncle."

"Excuse me?" said Michael.

"You're my mother's cousin," said Tracy. "Technically, that makes you my first cousin, once removed."

"You've been calling me Uncle Michael your whole life."

Tracy sighed, exasperated. "Can I go now? Please?"

Veronica waved her off as she curled up into the chair again. "Sooner you're finished," said Veronica, "sooner we can all get to bed."

And with that, Tracy picked up her milk crate and made her exit. But this time, she didn't hang around to eavesdrop. This time, she hurried up the stairs, taking them two at a time, and made straight for the dressing room, dropping the crate onto the props table along the way.

She rifled through the costume rack, searching for the outfit she'd hidden there, in plain sight, in a place neither mom would think to look. There was no telling how long it would take them all to clear out, but they wouldn't wait for her forever, and the chances of them coming up here instead of just calling for her—if they even bothered with that—were slim. So, she might as well get dressed, get ready.

Downstairs, a door opened. Tracy peeked out the window and saw Veronica, Michael, and Jenna step out onto the lawn. That was good. It was all good.

She changed, transformed herself. The stage blacks were balled up on the floor now, replaced with jeans that hugged her hips, a sweater that bared one shoulder, and a pair of sunglasses so big they gave her back a sense of mystery the other garments gave away.

"Sunglasses at night?" said Desiree, suddenly behind her.

"What?" said Tracy.

Desiree stood silent for a moment, sizing her up.

"What?" Tracy said again.

Desiree put a hand to her mouth and began to shake her head.

"What?"

"You're pregnant," said Desiree, falling backwards into a chair. "And don't lie. I can tell. I was with your mom when she found out she was pregnant with you."

"I'm not—"

"How did it happen? Did you use a condom? I mean, seriously, given the family history—"

"For serious, Des! I'm not," said Tracy, sitting now herself. "I'd cross my heart, but it's two sizes too small and awfully hard to find."

"Are you having sex?" said Desiree.

"And what if I was, Mother Abigail?"

"Who is Mother Abi—"

"Never mind," said Tracy. "Point is: I'm older than Mum was when Dad—"

"That man is not your father," said Desiree, leaning forward, shaking a finger at her, looking more like a mother than she ever had before. Every gray hair, all dozen or so of them, seemed to glint in the light as she shook that finger.

"I'm sorry," said Tracy, trying not to laugh at the beauty queen aging before her very eyes. "*The Runt*. I'm older than Mum was when the Runt knocked her up. And, anyway, I haven't had it yet. I'm just thinking about it."

"Well, stop thinking. It is way too early for you to—"

"This coming from the Handjob Queen of Roller Kingdom. Tell me again: how many pairs of leather pants did you stroke on metal night for free French fries?"

Desiree ducked her head. "We were stupid when we were kids," she said. "Our job as parents is to make sure you learn from our mistakes, not repeat them."

Tracy sighed a heavy sigh. "I did not choose wisely on this one," she said.

Desiree looked up again, her eyes wide, her jaw drooping. "You were going to tell me and not your mom?"

"That was the plan, Jan."

Desiree set a hand on Tracy's knee and squeezed. "You are too smart," she said, "and you know this family too well to think you can get away with secrets like that."

"I came to you because I thought you'd understand," said Tracy.

"No," said Desiree. "You came to me because you thought I'd give you permission."

And that was true. Desiree was the parent you brought your first speeding ticket to, the one you sought out at the mall when you wanted the credit card for something you didn't really need.

"This guy," said Tracy. "I don't want to marry him. I don't want to be with him forever. Hell, I might not even see him again after tonight. His family's just renting a place down here for the weekend. But I like him."

"That's fine," said Desiree. "Like him all you want. But from a distance. Pining's good for the soul. Getting pregnant at 18, not so much."

Tracy stood and stomped over to the other side of the room, aware, even as she stomped, of how childlike this response was, aware of how much this would just calcify Desiree's stance that she was too young. Aware, but too pissed off to care.

"Tracy," said Desiree. "Do you think you're on some kind of timeline here? Because you're not. You can... Waiting isn't... You..."

As Desiree trailed off, Tracy wanted to turn and see what clues the look on her face might give, but she also felt certain that now was the time to stand her ground.

"Your Uncle Michael was right," said Desiree. "There is definitely something weird in the air tonight."

"You know what?" said Tracy, giving in and turning, unable to bear the sound of that asshole's name without some kind of a response. "You know what?" she said. "Fuck Michael."

"Whoa," said Desiree, standing. "Hold on. That's your uncle you're talking about. He's the closest thing you have to a—"

"He is not my uncle. And he most certainly is not my father."

"Tracy," said Desiree, "where is all this coming from?"

Tracy thrust her hand toward the door, toward the props table just beyond it. "The boot," she said. "The goddamned boot!"

"The play?" said Desiree, looking confused.

"It's like he's wearing it one moment and then not wearing it the next."

"Okay," said Desiree, "now I'm lost."

"It's a metaphor," said Tracy. "The boot represents everything our family's struggled with for over a hundred and fifty years. It's the call to adventure, to danger, to frivolity, to the sea from whence we came. And you can either wear it or not wear it. You can't do both. But Michael? He wants to do both. And, maybe you can for a while. But you can't forever. Eventually, you've got to take it off or keep it on. Eventually, you've got to choose!"

"Okay," said Desiree. "Slow down."

"No," said Tracy. "I'm not slowing down. Not yet. It's my turn to wear it. And I'm going to wear the shit out of that boot until there's nothing left."

And with that, with nothing left to say, Tracy pushed past her stepmother and made for the stairs, for adventure and danger and frivolity, yes, but also for all of the other things that were waiting for her, the things she did not know and could not yet name.

❦ 3 ❦

They crept in through the side door a few hours later, Tracy and her two best friends in the world. Tana came first, buxom as Brünnhilde, with a voice to match, only the missing valkyrie's helmet keeping her from looking the spitting image of that archetypal fat lady. Then came Tori, a lean and sinewy Odette, a self-described ugly duckling that, now that she had the love of Tana, felt like the swan she dreamed of dancing on stage.

"So," said Tana, "where did whatshisname—"

"Tucker," said Tori.

"Where did Tucker run off to?"

It had all been going so well, from the moment he had pulled his parents' SUV into Tana's driveway to the moment, on their way back from Provincetown, when Tori had volunteered to take the wheel so that Tucker and Tracy could sit in the back. And then it had been going even better, in that backseat, as they drove home down Route 6, as they rolled by Tracy's house with the lights out and the car in neutral and parked down at Red River Beach. It had all been going so well, until:

"He forgot the condom," said Tracy.

"Oh my God," said Tana. "Seriously, you cannot do this."

"He went to go get it," said Tori. "It's not like she was going to—"

"No," said Tana. "She can't do it at all. If he's too dim to remember the condom—"

Tracy groaned, exasperated. "Has it occurred to you I picked him *because* he's dim?"

Tana sank into the center-stage chair, rolling her eyes. Tori still stood, dumbfounded. "Oh, Trace," she said, "that's not why, is it?"

"You're the smartest kid in our class," said Tana, "an amazing writer, and a sexy-ass bitch to boot. You deserve better than insert tab A into slot B."

Tracy sat on the coffee table, leveling with this girl she'd known since the move down the Cape all those years ago. "Yeah," she said, "well, if I don't start with tab A, I'm never going to get to X, Y, or Z now, am I?"

Tori asked, "Did you really pick him because he's dumb?"

"I picked him," said Tracy, "because he's here. And because he's not *from* here. Because he saw the sexy-ass bitch before the virtuous valedictorian."

Tana reached for Tracy's knee and squeezed. "Give someone some time and they'd see the sexy, too."

Tori sat behind Tracy on the table and wrapped her arms around her friend. "I mean," she said, "I understand where you're coming from, but—"

"Wait," said Tana. "How do *you* understand where she's coming from?"

"What I meant was—"

"We've been sleeping together," said Tana, "since the sixth grade."

"We were not 'sleeping together' back then," said Tori. "We were just sleeping together."

"Oh my god," said Tana. "Speaking of dim."

"Guys!" said Tracy. "Tucker and I is going to happen. Please get over it."

"Okay," said Tana, "fine. Your funeral. But where?"

"Where?" said Tracy.

"I believe," said Tori, "she wants to know which floor of the theater you'll be using, so that she and I can abscond to the other."

Tana smiled. "That would be correct."

"Of course," said Tori, leaning in closer to Tracy and whispering conspiratorially to her, "she's assuming I'm still going to give it up after she called me dim."

"But baby," said Tana, "your naïveté is one of the reasons I love you."

Tracy gave Tori's arms a squeeze and extricated herself from her friend's embrace. "We'll be down here," she said, standing.

"So," said Tana, "we can have the attic, with all the props and set pieces?"

"As long as you mind where you place those props," said Tracy. "You don't know where they've been."

Tana stood, extended a hand to Tori, and then dragged her off toward the stairs, the two of them pausing only long enough to each give Tracy a peck on the cheek, a silent wish of good luck. And then, then she was alone.

She was about to tidy up when she realized that all the tidying was done. So she paced instead, the sound of heels clicking against the floorboards keeping her company. It was such a strange sound, so disconnected from her understanding of herself. Tracy Silver didn't wear heels, especially heels that went click and clack. But, then again, she didn't wear jeans this tight either, or sweaters that showed off bare shoulders. And she didn't bite her nails, Ms. Tracy Silver, but here she was: biting them just the same.

Behind her, the outside door creaked open and the boy's voice called out, "Got it!"

Tucker was all muscle and hair gel, his body a carefully manufactured machine, his coiffure a calculated mess of brown hair. Only his glasses, square-rimmed and too hip for their own good, did anything to soften him. But that was okay. Tracy wasn't interested in anything or anyone soft, at least not tonight.

"You sure you didn't forget anything else?" she asked him.

"What else could I possibly forget?"

"I don't know," said Tracy. "You could be rocking a King Missle situation over there."

Tucker squinted. "A what?" he said.

"King Missle," said Tracy. "They had a song called 'Detachable P—.' Never mind."

Tucker nodded and headed for the chair, running a finger along it. "So," he said, inspecting his finger, as if for dust, "how was the play tonight?"

"The old man finally nailed his monologue," said Tracy.

"Which one?" said Tucker. "Doesn't he spend the whole play giving speeches?"

"The one at the end," said Tracy, "when he's strangling her."

"Oh yeah," he said, sitting in the chair, then propping his feet up on the table. "That was awesome."

"Excuse me?" said Tracy. "What is awesome about him choking the life out of the mother of his child?"

Tucker laughed. "But it ain't his kid; it's the demon's. Right?"

"If you believe the demon was real and not a figment of his psychotic imagination."

Tucker laughed again. "Oh, that demon was real, alright. Did you see the size of his—"

"I did," said Tracy, cutting him off. "But whatevs. What was so awesome about Silas killing Ada?"

"It was the passion in his eyes," said Tucker. "The only other time he looked that into something was when he walked in reading Shakespeare."

Tracy said nothing, not because there was nothing to say, but because he was right and she couldn't bear to concede the point. Though she supposed she was conceding, just by being silent. And so, maybe—but she cut herself off and went back to listening to him before she could finish the thought.

"That was the scene where I first noticed you," Tucker was saying, "lurking in the shadows, a death stare on your face. You may have hated him, but you were into it too. There was some part of him you liked, despite yourself."

Tracy stomped over to him, straddled him, and then pressed her face toward his, ready to kiss him when he said:

"Shit! I just remembered the other thing I forgot."

"What?" she said.

"My car," he said. "I forgot to lock it."

She ran her hands along his shoulders, let a few fingers slip under his neckline. "You're fine," she told him. "The hooligans of Harwich are fast asleep by now."

"It's my parents' car," he said. "I gotta go check. If it got stolen—"

She stood and moved out of his way, then watched him go. "Girls!" she shouted, once he was gone.

There was a rush of footsteps overhead and then Tana and Tori appeared in the doorway once more. Tracy stifled a laugh at the sight of them, and actually had to turn away to hold herself together. Tana was dressed in a devil's costume, Tori in an angel's. Tracy cast a glance over each shoulder to see if they were in the right places, then joked:

"I'm having a total *Animal House* moment here."

"*Animal House?*" said Tori, standing off to the left.

Tana chortled, getting it, then said, "Fuck him. Fuck his brains out. Suck his dick. Squeeze his buns. You know he wants it."

Tori said, "I thought I was the one advocating for this hook up."

"*Animal House*, darlin'. I'm just playing the part I'm dressed for," said Tana.

"I thought you guys were headed for the attic," said Tracy.

"We were," said Tori, "but when we passed the costume racks on the second floor, Miss Thing couldn't resist."

"Cosplay pushes my buttons," said Tana. "Sue me! We're in a theater."

Tracy sighed. "What am I going to do?" she said, as she turned to face them.

"Do?" said Tana. "You're going to *do* him. You wanted adventure. He'll give you a good ride, at the very least."

Tori rolled her eyes. "How can you tell?"

"He's an idiot," said Tana. "He can't carry on a conversation about anything other than sportsball. So, he's got to be good at something. Right?"

"Right," said Tracy, nodding as if she were sure.

The outside door creaked open again and Tucker crept back in. He looked as if he were about to say something, then paused and simply smiled at the sight before him.

"We'll be up in the attic," said Tori. "First and second floor are all yours."

The girls slipped upstairs while Tucker drew ever closer.

"So," he said, "what's it going to be? The halo or the horns?"

Tracy put a finger to his lips to shush him. "Please stop talking," she said, taking his hand in her own, "before I change my mind."

And, because he was obedient, because he wanted his bone, so to speak, he didn't say another word. Not one, not until she begged him to say her name and he said it.

Again and again.

❧ 4 ❧

They slept on the ratty taupe loveseat that was tucked into the alcove beside the lighting booth. Many a technician had napped here during tech week and many an actor had fucked here during cast parties (or at least those were the stories she'd heard). But this was the first time Tracy had been on this couch in years, and she didn't understand how anyone could even sit on the collapsing old thing, let alone perform some other more vigorous act. It was true that they, both of them, had slept on it, but only Tucker was still asleep. Tracy's rest had been fitful at best.

But maybe it wasn't even the love seat's fault. Maybe it was the fact that his chest, so pleasing in its hardness when looked upon, didn't make a great pillow. Or maybe it was the layer of sweat between them that kept drying then coming back, drying then coming back. Or the ache between her legs. Or the place where her groin clung to his hip, all sticky, as if her labia didn't want to let go. Was that her, the stickiness? It must've been, right? Because the condom had worked; she'd seen how he'd filled it. Whatever substance it was that glued them together, she had made it.

But what did that mean? That she wanted him again? Because she didn't. She knew that now. She didn't regret the one time. No, no, that had been fun, if a bit awkward, if a bit painful. But she didn't want to do it again. She was glad he'd only brought one condom, despite the gentle kiss she'd given him when, after they were done, he lamented his decision not to bring more.

Tracy crawled out from under him, the sounds of their bodies parting louder than she'd imagined they'd be, louder than she could stomach. Her tummy turned and she braced herself against the wall, her legs wobbling. But the moment passed and soon she was standing up just fine, searching the floor for her underwear, her bra, her jeans.

She was dressed except for her top when, beyond the curtain that hid the alcove, she heard the outside door open. She tried not to breathe, but that only made every breath sound louder. Tracy heard footsteps headed for the stage as she peeked from behind the curtain to see who it was. But before she could see him, she could hear him.

It was Michael, with headphones on, singing.

Tracy put a hand over Tucker's mouth and nudged him awake. His eyes shot open in panic, then quickly narrowed as he listened to Tracy's instructions. He nodded along, looked calm. It was almost as if he'd been through this routine before.

While he dressed, Tracy stepped up into the lighting booth, climbed the ladder that led to the second floor, and peered through the darkness for any sight of the girls. As luck would have it, they were creeping down from the attic at that very moment, back in their street clothes.

"Is someone singing down there?" whispered Tana.

Tracy nodded, put a finger to her lips.

They drew closer.

"You have a plan?" whispered Tori.

Tracy nodded again. "You guys go and wait by the stage-right alcove; Tucker's over in the stage-left one. When I give the signal—"

"What signal?" said Tana.

"I'm going to throw on one of the lights to disorient him." said Tracy. "As soon as you see it, you run. Tucker's going to do the same."

They nodded in agreement, then took their places. Tracy ducked out of the booth to give Tucker a thumbs up.

"Will I see you again?" said Tucker.

Tracy shrugged. "It's a mystery," she said, quoting from a favorite film, though one he'd probably never seen. She was about to joke with him and say "Places," but she figured he wouldn't know what that meant either. So, she simply waved him goodbye and slipped back into the booth.

It was hard to see where Michael was in the darkness, with nary a work light to illuminate him. But then, out of nowhere, the screen of his phone lit up his face. It was perfect. He was standing right beneath the special that was set to illuminate the center-stage chair. Tracy flipped on the lighting board, waited a second to hear the tell-tale hum of the instruments overhead, then threw up the slider for the special.

A harsh circle of bright white light shone down on Michael out of the darkness and he looked up at the sight of it, startled. On cue, Tana and Tori booked it past him. Then Tucker did the same. Michael spun around to see who was racing by, but he was squinting and probably—*hopefully*—unable to pick out a face from the darkness.

Once her friends were clear, Tracy slid up the work lights, a gentle purple wash filling out the darkness around Michael. She crouched down and threw open the cooler the tech kept back in the booth for drinks, searching for the nip bottle she'd stashed there. It was time. There was no denying that now. Tiny bottle in hand, she found her sweater, put it on, and stepped out toward the stage.

Michael, mug in hand, shook his head at her as she drew closer.

"Isn't it a little early for your morning cocoa?" she asked him.

"Isn't it a little late for you to be sneaking around?"

"Touché," she said.

He set down his mug and began to wrap his headphones around his phone. "I couldn't sleep," he said. "What's your excuse?"

She almost told him. A few months ago, before she'd seen what she'd seen, Michael was almost on par with Desiree in the cool parental figure department. But not anymore. No, instead of telling him, she pled the fifth.

"Fair enough," he said.

"So, what'd you think of the play?" she asked him, looking for a way to distract him, to get closer to the mug without him noticing.

"I enjoyed it," he said. "It was helpful."

"Helpful?" she said, circling, trying to see if he would counter. "How so?"

"Well, it was about my great-grandfather, wasn't it? I always wanted to know how our family got so fucked up, and now I know."

"Well," she said, "only some of the story was verifiable fact. Uncle Matt embellished the rest."

"Oh, so he's still Uncle Matt, is he?"

Man, he was insufferable. Tracy sighed, then said, "Seeing as he's actually my mother's brother and not just her cousin, yes."

"Semantics," said Michael, still not moving, still not turning away.

Get him talking about the play, she thought. *Get him pontificating. He'll pace. You'll get your chance.*

She asked, "How much did you know about Old Silas before seeing the play?"

"The basics," he said. "I knew he was a Civil War vet, that he married a whole bunch of times before he met my great-grandmother, that he was in his seventies when they tied the knot. I knew he was an asshole to his two kids."

"What did you know about the boot?" she asked.

"Not a lot," he said. "And I still don't get why it was so important."

He didn't get why it was so important?!? How could he say that he finally understood how the family got fucked up without also understanding the metaphor of the boot?

"The boot was a metaphor?" he asked.

Shit, she thought. *How much of that did I say out loud?*

"For what?" he said.

"God," she said, "you really are hopeless."

"OK then, Ms. Valedictorian, illuminate your poor, uneducated uncle."

She sat on the table, beside the mug, exasperated. And then, when she realized where she'd sat—beside it instead of in front of it—she was even angrier. A few inches to the left and she could have done the deed behind her back before he was any the wiser.

"The boot belonged to his father," she said, "a mariner who preferred the adventure of the sea to the quiet comforts of his family."

"Yes," he said, "I knew that."

"When his father drowned at sea, the boot was all that washed ashore. It was a warning, but it was also a promise."

"A promise of what?" said Michael.

"A promise of possibility without boundaries, of—"

"Death isn't a boundary?"

"You know what I mean?"

"I don't think I do," said Michael.

Tracy rose, looked him in the eye. She said, "Our family broke and continues to break because we can't make choices. We want the adventure the boot promises, but we also want the safety that comes when the boot is under the bed instead of on our foot."

"I don't think that's fair," said Michael. "To your mom, or to anyone else who—"

"This isn't about my mom," she said. "This is about you."

Bingo! That got him, hurt him. He glared at her for a moment, his eyes wide. His lips trembled, the corners of them twitching, as if caught between a smirk and a frown.

He asked, "You don't think I've made choices in my life?"

"I know you haven't," she said. "I know you can't."

He made to open his mouth and say something, but then seemed to stop himself short. Then, he walked toward the exit, mumbling, "You have no idea, kid. No idea."

While his back was turned to her, Tracy slipped the nip bottle out of her pocket, unscrewed its cap, and poured its contents into his mug. She gave the mug a swirl, pocketed the empty bottle, and then said, "Don't forget your mug."

Michael turned around, faced her again. "My mug?" he said.

"Yeah," she said, "I'm done cleaning up in here for the night."

He came back to the table, picked up the mug, and took a swig.

"Does it really help you relax?" she said. "The cocoa?"

"I wake up pretty panicky, most mornings. This has always done the trick."

She smiled, gave a light laugh. "Chocolate always hypes me up," she said.

"Don't I know it?" he said. "All the times I babysat you as a kid..." He trailed off, sipped at his cocoa again. "You really think I can't make choices?"

"Don't beat yourself up," said Tracy. "Mom couldn't either, not until she had that *Christmas Carol* dream of hers."

Michael chuckled. "I'll never forget when she told me about that. Sounded like she was high as a kite. But whatever the three spirits showed her, it did the trick. Within a year, she and the Runt were through and she and Desiree were together at last."

Tracy slipped her phone out of her pocket, checked the time, and then said, "She had a little help getting that dream going, I have to admit."

"What do you mean?" said Michael.

"Well, Uncle Matt was getting sick of hearing her bitch about her plight, so one night he asked me to slip a little something into her evening tea. I was young and angry and he promised it would make things better, so..." She trailed off, waiting for him to catch on.

"Really?" said Michael. "He did that? You were, what, seven or eight? What was it?"

"An old family recipe," said Tracy. "Or, well, it was something one of Old Silas' wives cooked up. The Wiccan. The one he strangled to death in the play.

Michael shook his head, finished his cocoa, and set it down on the table again. Tracy checked her phone. It was almost time.

"Christ," said Michael, "I can't believe he got you involved in that."

"It was all for the best," said Tracy.

"Yeah," he said, "because she was going to sleep. But what if she'd gotten up in the middle of the night?"

"I don't know," she said, showing him the nip bottle. " I guess we're going to find out."

"Tracy," he said, rubbing his stomach, then clutching it as he winced. "What did you..."

He stumbled as he came toward her, tried to steady himself on the chair. But it was no use. *O true apothecary*! she thought. *Thy drugs are quick*.

"I know the truth about you," she told him, as he began to twitch. "It's time to make sure you know it, too."

From the second floor, she brought mannequins. From the attic, she brought a table, chairs, and props. And then, once everything was set, she went back to the lighting booth. From the cooler, she withdrew another nip bottle, with a less potent brew, and she downed that herself. She had to drink it quick. It was the only way, according to Ada's notes, to induce a collective hallucination, to join Michael on the trip which he was about to take.

When she began to see things out there on the stage herself, things that weren't there but were, she lay her hands upon the lighting board and got the show on the road.

T he courtroom was a sort of mashup. On the one hand, it looked the trial scene from *The Undiscovered Country*, Michael's favorite Star Trek film: a big circular room with a beam of light shining down on the platform where stood the accused. But, on the other hand, it was too colorful to be Klingon. The jury, seated all around them, was comprised of every female comic book, cartoon, science fiction, or fantasy character Michael had ever crushed on, each of them done up in the most audacious outfit they'd ever been seen in. They all looked annoyed to be there, everyone from Slave Leia to *Little House*'s Laura Ingalls, from The Little Mermaid to *Lost*'s Charlotte Lewis. There were six copies of Scarlett Johansson seated behind seven variations of the X-Men's Jean Grey. And Dana Scully was there too, chatting it up with what looked like a Vulcan and looking quite pleased to be rid of Mulder for the evening. *God*, Tracy thought, as she looked around, *I have never seen so many redheads in one place*.

Michael was still out cold, though clad now in an orange jumpsuit. *Fitting*, Tracy thought, given that orange was Michael's favorite color. She thought of how happy he'd be, under different circumstances, to have found something to wear in that shade besides his ratty old Reese's t-shirt.

And what was she wearing, Tracy wondered, looking herself over. Judge's robes, of course. Simple black. Nothing crazy. No powdered wig, or anything like that. She sat behind a tall podium, looming high above the scene, like the Queen of Hearts in *Alice in Wonderland*. A banner hung down the front of the bench, a rather severe looking Venus symbol stitched into it.

Tracy took up her gavel and banged it down three times. "All rise!" she called out. And when Michael still did not stir, she waved to the shadows at the foot of her bench and two bailiffs stepped out, one done up like a swordswoman of old, the other like a gunslinger from beyond the apocalypse. The two women pulled Michael to his feet as Tracy repeated herself: "I said, 'All rise!'"

Michael squeezed his eyes together, shaking his head. "Where am I?" he said.

"Michael Silver," said Tracy, "you are on trial for your crimes against femininity."

"On trial for what?"

Tracy smirked down at him. "Anything you say can and will be held against you in this court. So, we recommend you shut up."

"If this is a trial," said Michael, "where is the jury? Where are the lawyers?"

"This is your courthouse," said Tracy, waving her gavel around, urging him to see for himself. "You built it, brick by brick. So, you tell me."

He said nothing for a minute, as he looked around, locking eyes with several of the women his subconscious had invited to render his verdict. His jaw went slack, his lower lip drooping. Tracy couldn't tell if he was staring in disbelief, or if he was ogling them.

"You're the judge?" he said, still not looking at her.

"Apparently," she said. "And, if you don't mind, I'd like to call my next witness."

Now he looked. "Wait," he said, "the judge doesn't call witnesses."

"In here she does," said the two bailiffs.

Tracy was amused by this. All the power rested with her, except for the final judgment. And maybe that was her call, too. After all, the jury was fiction; she was reality.

"OK, fine," said Michael. "But don't you mean first witness, not next?"

She wasn't sure what she meant, so she embellished: "We're halfway through this trial already, Mr. Silver. Have you been asleep this whole time? Is this matter not worthy of your attention? Did you not see me, right here in front of you?"

"No," said Michael. "I, uh..."

"How typical," said Tracy.

"How unsurprising," said the bailiffs.

"Tracy!" shouted Michael. "Wait a minute. I—"

But Tracy ignored him. She looked down at the notes in front of her, scribbled so many days ago now, back when the potion was still brewing, when it wasn't even certain when Michael would be in town, when it seemed like there would be more time to plan, more time to prepare the case. Tracy looked at the notes and saw her mother's name—Veronica—and that's who she called first.

In the real world, she felt her hand sliding up the fader for a second pool of light, off to the left, but she didn't see the mannequin there that she was expecting. She saw Veronica, a younger Veronica, five and a half months pregnant, in a godawful prom dress the color of a pistachio. Tracy closed her eyes, tried to remember what was real, and then looked down. There was no fader anymore. There was nothing more real than the young woman beside her, nothing closer to the truth than the gavel in her hand.

"Please," Tracy said to Veronica, "state your name for the record."

"Veronica Amelia Silver," said the young woman—younger, Tracy realized, than she was herself.

"And what," said Tracy, "is your relationship to the accused?"

"I'm his cousin," said Veronica.

"Could you please explain the scene we are about to see?"

"Scene?" said Michael. "Is this a courthouse or a playhouse?"

Tracy realized how preposterous it sounded, but scene was what she had meant to say, what she felt compelled to say. She pointed down at him with her gavel. "The accused will remain silent until spoken to."

"This is absurd!" said Michael.

"Guards?" said Tracy.

The Gunslinger drove the butt of her rifle into Michael's stomach, and he fell to his knees. Then the Swordswoman grabbed a fistful of his hair and yanked his head backward. She put her sword to his throat.

"The accused will remain silent until spoken to," said Tracy. "Do you understand."

Still on his knees, Michael nodded. A drop of blood traced its way down his neck, from the edge of the blade and onto the collar of his jumpsuit.

"Ms. Silver," said Tracy, "please continue."

"This was the night of our prom," she said, and suddenly it was, the courtroom replaced with a school gymnasium all done up in maroon and white, the DJ playing a schizophrenic mix of Nirvana and Michael Jackson. "I didn't want to go," said Veronica, "but my dad didn't give me a choice. He decided it would be best for the family's good name if I went with the baby's father, my soon-to-be husband, to keep up appearances."

Out of the darkness beside Veronica appeared Tracy's father, the Runt, dressed in a tuxedo, a green cummerbund at his waist to complement the dress of the awkward girl beside him. They looked so strange, so young. Not that they were old now—they were the youngest parents in her grade, in fact—but the idea of them creating her this early in their lives was harder to stomach in reality than it had been in theory. Even the photo albums didn't do this scene justice. Somehow, by the time it came time for photographs, the two of them would figure a way to at least look like they liked each other. But now, standing on the edge of the dance floor, not quite an arm's length apart, his hands clasped behind his back, hers folded underneath her breasts and above her belly, they looked like they had never touched each other before, let alone touched enough to—

Tracy shook her head to rid the thought from her mind.

"Meanwhile," said Veronica, "the person I wanted to be with, Desiree, wasn't going to go at all."

"But she did go," said Tracy, "didn't she?"

"Yes," said Veronica. "At the last minute, my cousin Michael asked her."

Michael stood, shrugging off the bailiffs as if they were ghosts, which is what they seemed to be now. He looked all about the room, searching, it seemed, for Desiree.

"And she said yes?" asked Tracy.

"Yes," said Veronica.

"Ms. Silver, is it true that your cousin was a freshman on the night in question?"

"Yes," said Veronica.

Tracy scribbled on her notepad, pencil scratches echoing through the chamber. "Do you have any idea then," she began, "why Desiree, cheerleading captain, star of the field hockey squad, lusted after by hundreds of her schoolmates, would deign to accept Mr. Silver's invitation?"

Veronica looked over at Michael, who was still looking around for Desiree. She shook her head, sighed, and then said, "She felt sorry for him."

"Why?" said Tracy.

"Because," said Michael, still looking, about to step from his circle of light, "because I'd had a crush on her from the moment I first met her."

"Mr. Silver," said Tracy, "I will not warn you again. I'm not interested in your version of things, however truthful you might swear it to be, whatever excuses you might have for—"

From the shadows came Desiree's voice. "Let him tell the story," she said.

Tracy had heard it all before, the awkward circumstances under which Veronica's cousin had once crushed on her future wife. Back in the day, Michael swore he was in love with Desiree. At fourteen, maybe he didn't know what love was, but he knew for sure that he felt something. And it wasn't just 'the hots.' He had more than just 'the hots' for her. As his grandfather had so eloquently put it, at that year's Christmas party, Michael lit up like Rudolph's nose at the mere sight of Desiree. And if that wasn't love, then what the heck was it?

What was it about Desiree, in Michael's opinion, that made her so combustible? Well, you had to look at it this way: she was a senior, and a cheerleader, and far prettier than any cover girl he'd ever seen, and yet, despite all that, Desiree still said "hi" to him in the hallways at school. She was Veronica's friend—what a fucking idiot he was, Tracy thought, if he didn't see they were more than that—and that meant she knew Michael by proxy, and kinda-sorta had to be cordial to him when they bumped into each other at parties and whatnot. But she was under no obligation to acknowledge his existence within the hallowed halls of the high school. And even if she was so obligated, she surely wasn't required to give him a smile on occasion, or a wave. Acknowledging a freshman's existence, let alone a freshman boy's existence, was tantamount to social suicide. And yet—

Desiree danced with him now, stunning the room in her scarlet satin shift. "I didn't go to prom with you because I felt sorry for you," she said. "I said yes because I wanted to put a smile on someone's face, and if it couldn't be Veronica's, if it couldn't be mine, then why not yours? You were always so sweet."

"Objection!" shouted Tracy, ready to hurl her gavel at the pair of them.

"Tracy," said Veronica, off dancing with the Runt now, making a fool of her pregnant-ass self. "Give him a chance to defend himself."

"No!" said Tracy. "I will not. That's all he ever does: defend himself. All those pre-emptive strikes to keep us feeling sorry for him and stop us from asking the difficult questions. Like this one," she said. "Mr. Silver, do you recall where you were on the night of December 31, 1991?"

Michael ducked his head. In shame, Tracy happened to know.

"Where were you?" said Desiree.

"I repeat," said Tracy, "do you recall where you were on the night of December 31, 1991?"

"I was at home," said Michael, still not looking up, which was even more incriminating than perhaps he realized, since his eyes were now focused squarely on Desiree's chest. "I was at home," he said again. "In bed."

"And do you recall what you were doing that night," said Tracy, "alone and in bed?"

"I plead the fifth," he said.

"There is no fifth to plead here," said Tracy. "You will answer the question!"

"I was jerking off, alright?"

"To what?" said Tracy.

"To a picture of Desiree," said Michael, "from the yearbook."

Tracy knew just what picture it was, the page dog-eared in Michael's copy of the yearbook, which he'd given to Veronica and Desiree as a wedding present after learning they'd both burned theirs in grief during the years of their separation. The photo was of Desiree in her field hockey uniform, smiling for one of the many cameras that followed her that year—one of the guys on the school newspaper took it upon himself to get a photo of her into every issue, even if there was no legitimate reason to do so. She had her white shirt on, her plaid skirt, and her knee socks of course, and every piece of her ensemble was a bit dirty, as if she'd just finished up a game. But the pièce de résistance was the hockey stick she clutched to her chest, between her breasts to a certain extent, a happy accident that had been the impetus for many happy "accidents" on the part of Mr. Michael Silver and his perverted fourteen-year-old imagination.

"It's okay," said Desiree, blushing, smiling, lifting his face up by the chin.

"It is not okay!" said Tracy. "Mr. Silver, are you aware of where Desiree and your cousin Veronica were that night?"

"Tracy," said Veronica, "what does the one thing have to do with the other?"

"Mr. Silver," said Tracy, "are you aware?"

All at once, the dancing stopped, the lights faded, and the record stopping spinning.

"I am," said Michael, walking away from Desiree.

"Where were they?" said Tracy.

Michael looked over his shoulder. Veronica and Desiree were side by side now. "They were at a party," said Michael, "at Veronica's house. They were drinking and playing spin the bottle."

"And?" said Tracy.

Michael looked away from them again, staring off into the distance as he said, "After Veronica spun the bottle and it landed on Desiree, it caused quite a ruckus. They kissed, and that was enough to cause all of the hornballs at the table to pair off."

"And did Veronica and Desiree pair off?"

"No," said Michael. "They didn't."

"Objection!" said Veronica. "Relevance?"

"Overruled," said Tracy.

"Tracy," said Desiree, "what is the point of this?"

"The point," said Tracy, "is that your quote-unquote sweet

prom date was no better than the hornball who took you to bed that night, no better than the runt who got my mother pregnant. And yet, he consistently tries to pass himself off as sensitive and—"

"No," said Desiree, storming back toward Michael, the lights and the band and the crowd returning as she did. "Do you know what he said to me that night? Prom night?"

"Thank you for saying yes," said Michael, as they began to dance again.

"I'm having a great time," said Desiree.

"It must suck," he said, "to see her with him."

They both glanced over at Veronica, who stood against the far wall, nodding along as she listened to the Runt. She tried to get a word in, but failed.

"I don't know what you mean," said Desiree.

Michael said, "I know how much you both like—"

"You're wrong," said Desiree, cutting him off. "I don't know where you got that idea."

"I'm not wrong," he said. "I'm a details guy. You've seen how long it takes me to get anything done. That mural down the hall, the one with the lions chasing the Indians, I obsessed over that for months."

"And?" said Desiree.

Tracy watched him swallow, as if trying to build up some head of steam inside himself to say what needed to be said. For a moment, she saw her uncle again, the man she wanted him to be, the man he was capable of being: a man who said the right thing, who did the right thing. Always.

"And," he said, "I've been obsessing over you for years. I see the way you and Veronica look at each other. And I've seen the way she looks at the Runt. It may take her a while to see what she's seeing, but she will. Eventually," he said, "she won't be able to ignore it."

Desiree ducked her head and nodded. "You're a pretty smart kid," she said.

"Thanks," he said.

Desiree kissed Michael on the cheek and pulled him into a hug. They danced close for a second before Tracy felt the anger swelling in her again, saw the Michael in this moment that she needed to purge, to wipe away. His hand was on Desiree's back, her lower back, not quite where it wasn't supposed to be yet, but getting there.

"The witnesses are excused," said Tracy.

Desiree and Michael parted ever so slightly. They smiled at each other, kept dancing, as if waiting to see how long the moment would last. Waiting to see how long Tracy would *let* it last.

"Guards," said Tracy. "Separate them."

The bailiffs pulled them apart, the Gunslinger shunting Desiree off toward Veronica, the Swordswoman shoving Michael back onto the stand of the accused, all light going out except for the circle that shone down on him from above.

Ｈigh atop the judge's bench, Tracy was anxious to get on with things. She was on a roll, and Michael was reeling, so as soon as Desiree and Veronica were gone, Tracy said, "The prosecution calls its next—"

"That's it?" said Michael. "No breaks? No res—"

Tracy nodded into the darkness, where she saw light glint off a gun barrel. The Gunslinger stepped from the shadows, slammed her rifle into Michael's head once more, and laughed as he fell to his knees.

Satisfied, Tracy continued. "We call Robin Gates to the stand," she said.

Michael's head snapped up, his eyes still watering, a rivulet of blood on his chin, dripping down from where he'd bitten his lip. "Well that's not possible," he said. "She's... she's..."

Dead was what he meant to say. As a doornail. Just like Marley. Tracy held back a chuckle at the thought. Five years she'd been gone, compared with Marley's seven, and she looked much better than Scrooge's old partner ever had, as if those extra two years were when all the decay happened. No rotting teeth on her, nor crossed eyes, nor festering wounds held together by filthy rags.

And, as far as chains went, there were only the ones she wore in life. No, the Robin Gates that walked into their courtroom was like no ghost Tracy had ever seen. She was the spitting image of the girl Michael had fallen for all those years ago, the girl on his best friend's porch, the one he'd painted and drawn again and again.

She looked cold, her thin body shuddering as if still held in the grip of that steady January breeze they'd met in. And she looked just like the pixie Michael had always painted her to be. It wasn't just the way she carried herself, as if, like a bird, her bones were hollow and full of air, as if she might fly away at any moment. It was her hair, too—the short, chunky, playful cut of it. It was her bright, mischievous eyes. And it was the fact that it seemed as if the only things weighing her down at all were the jewelry that she wore, and the leather.

There were earrings everywhere, one dangly one in each lobe, two studs in each as well, and one up near the top of her right ear, right in the crook of a fleshy part, a puncture that made Tracy swoon for a moment at the sight of it. When Robin laughed, Tracy spied a stud splitting through the middle of her tongue. Michael, down below, searching for somewhere else to look, besides her eyes, besides her plunging neckline, seemed to have found the final piercing, or at least the final visible one, a small jewel lanced through the flesh above her navel.

"Ms. Gates," said Tracy, "what is your relationship to the accused?"

"Well," said Robin, fixated on Michael and not on Tracy, "for a period of approximately three years, I fucked his brains out on a regular basis."

Tracy banged her gavel down, half-amused and half-annoyed. She liked this girl, always had, and she thought she might miss Robin almost as much as Michael did. "Language," said Tracy, admonishing her.

"Which one?" said Robin.

"Excuse me?" said Tracy.

"Which language would you prefer?" said Robin. "I can do French—*J'ai baisé le cerveau hors de sa tête*—or German—*Ich sein Gehirn aus dem Kopf gefickt*. My Swedish is a little rusty, but I could give it a whirl."

Tracy said, "What I meant was—"

"Oh," said Robin, cutting her off. "I got it. *Jag knullade hans hjärna ut!*"

"If we could keep the vulgarity to a minimum," said Tracy, "that would be most appreciated."

Robin laughed, finally looking up at Tracy. "Well," she said, "fuck me in the ass and call me Charlie, I'll sure as shit do my goddamned best."

Once upon a time, she had been called—by the *Phoenix*, no less—"Boston's most notorious rock and roll slut." The mouth on her, Tracy now remembered, was a big part of why.

Tracy looked down at her notes again, trying not to get starstruck by this girl she'd spent her adolescence idolizing. She continued: "You were Mr. Silver's girlfriend from January 1995 through January 1998, is that correct?"

"Oui, oui," said Robin.

"And together you made up two thirds of the popular local band Gideon's Bible?"

"Well," said Robin, "at the beginning, technically speaking, we were one half of the band. But, you know, love triangles and all that."

Tracy knew that. How had she forgotten that? Or had she forgotten? Maybe when she'd written the question down she'd simply been trying for simplification. Maybe—she cut herself off and asked her next question: "Could you describe how you came to be involved with Mr. Silver?"

"Could I?" said Robin. "Man, I remember the night I met Michael Silver so well it hurts."

Tracy listened as she told the story, the third most recounted love story in their house, just after the story of her two moms getting together and the story of Michael and Jenna. They were headed to a Nine Inch Nails concert at the Centrum, Robin and David (the corner of the love triangle since lost to history), and in walked their ride, Michael, a guy in paint-stained jeans and a torn Voltron t-shirt, looking all innocent and unkempt, like he had no idea what he was in for. The way Robin used to tell it, he was the best kind of handsome: the kind that doesn't know it yet, and maybe never will.

"And it was at the concert that he made his move?" said Tracy.

"The concert?" said Robin. "I haven't even gotten there yet."

"We don't require every detail," said Tracy, which was true, though secretly she loved every one of them, from the crazed teenagers leaping over their heads to get to the mosh pit below, to Michael and Robin singing to each other of the tainted touch of each other's caress.

"Well, listen," said Robin, "Ms. Judge, Jury, and Executioner, you need to pipe the fuck down. I'm telling a story here."

"That's not how this works," said Tracy.

"I don't care how this works," said Robin. "This is how it *should* work. You argue against him, someone gets to counter. Basics of academic discourse, baby."

"I understand that," said Tracy. "I'm the valedictorian of—"

Robin shouted, "I'm the valedictorian of life, sweetheart!" and it was as if the judge's bench shrunk as a result, shriveled up a bit, tucked itself closer to the ground. "I know what's what," said Robin. "So, sit down and shut the fuck up for a while."

Tracy stared at Robin and Robin stared back. Robin seemed to be waiting, to see if Tracy would interrupt again. And only after a full measure of silence did she continue.

She talked about the car he drove, a gray Ford Tempo that was falling apart in every way imaginable. She lingered over the lights on the dash that were illuminated when they shouldn't have been, over the noises coming from places that should have been silent.

And then she talked about how none of it mattered once they were on the open road, how the stereo drowned out all that was wrong in the world, how they sang along to anything and everything.

Robin knelt down beside Michael now. "And you could sing," she said. "Oh, man, could you sing. Your voice was heavy, and warm, and untrained, and when you hit a note you didn't hit it because it was what you were taught to do. You hit that note because it felt right, because it felt good."

"You can't be here," said Michael, his hand creeping toward her cheek, as if to see if she was real. "You..." he said, pulling his hand back, wrapping his arms around his body, shaking his head. "You're—"

But Robin put two fingers to his lips to quiet him.

"Do you remember the concert?" she asked him.

"How could I forget it?" he said. "So many people were rushing to the floor that security lost control. The railings started to buckle."

"It was amazing," said Robin.

"It was," said Michael.

"And then," said Robin, "do you remember afterwards, when I made *my* move?"

Tracy caught the emphasis, rolled her eyes at it. Yes, technically, Robin had made the first move. But his eyes, the way he looked at her, the way he looked at Desiree—the way he looked at every woman, dammit—they proved that he was just as much at fault.

At fault for what? asked a voice in her brain, a voice she silenced with a shake of her head. *You know what*, she thought to herself.

Michael stood and walked away from Robin, the room transforming into the hall outside the auditorium. It was a zoo of people in black t-shirts and fishnet stockings, their mopey make-up ruined by sweat and post-show smiles.

Robin said, "Good show, huh? They play everything you wanted to hear?"

"I was hoping they'd do 'Heresy,'" said Michael. "It's become my, sort-of... I don't know... my anthem?"

Robin smiled, drawing nearer to him. "God is dead, huh?"

Michael ranted for a minute about how that wasn't what the singer was really saying, how the song was really more about why God sucked. He quoted lines, talked about the presence of the capital H in the song, and Robin ate it up, sauntering up to him, nodding along.

"You're really into it," she said. "I like that."

And then it was his story about his grandfather, the one who'd died the spring before, the first death he'd ever experienced for himself as a grown-up. *Blah, blah, blah.* That was Michael for you, co-opting family tragedies to explain his wild mood swings and his sudden changes in musical taste.

He coughed a little at the end of his monologue and that was when Robin did it, when she sealed the deal. She leaned in toward him, tilting her head, and pressed her lips to his Adam's apple, lingering there for a moment, puckering as she withdrew, as if to suck away the hurt with her as she stepped back.

"All better?" she said.

Michael turned away from her, and Tracy was startled by what happened next. And equally startled that she hadn't noticed it before. The room changed when he decided it should change. Michael was just as much in control as she was. They were back in the courthouse, the jury murmuring all around them, the bailiffs whispering something to each other too.

"Yes," said Michael, "it was all better. Except for the part where I lost my oldest friend over you. Except for the part where you cheated on me with that drummer you met at Berklee."

Robin squeezed his bicep, such as it was. "You do know it wasn't just that drummer?" she said. And then she rattled off the list: the slam poet from Maine, the part-time DJ at BCN, the bi drag queen from Swarthmore, and, of course, the twins from Wellesley.

"They didn't count," said Michael.

"Why," said Robin, "because they were chicks?"

"No," said Michael, "because that was our autumn of anything goes."

"Oh yeah," said Robin.

"Objection," said Tracy. "You're skipping ahead."

Robin scoffed: "I thought you wanted us to skip ahead."

"Only in the places I tell you to," said Tracy.

"Fine," said Michael, standing beside Robin, the two of them a united front now. "Where do you want us to go back to?"

Tracy consulted her notes, though she already knew the part she wanted to hear. "Your first time," she said, more timidly than she wished she had.

"The first time we did what?" said Robin. "The first time I blew him?"

Michael blushed, ducked his head.

"Because," said Robin, "that was a totally different time than the first time he ate me out, which was up in his room while you and the rest of the family were downstairs watching the Pops play the '1812 Overture.'"

Robin turned and squeezed Michael's arm with two hands now. "Do you remember," she said, "how I came in time with the cannon blasts? It was a good thing they had the sound blaring—"

Tracy slammed her gavel against its sounding block, cracking the block in two. She looked down at it, unsure how she'd done it. She was angry, yes, but they weren't even to the part that pissed her off the most. Maybe the stories of their escapades were swaying her, like the always did, convincing her that Michael was just being Michael. Maybe these old stories were doing more harm than good when it came to making her case against him.

"Ms. Gates," said Tracy, after a moment, "I'm not entirely sure we need any more of your testimony. If you can't control yourself, then you'll have to head straight back to where you came from. Is that what you want?"

Robin looked sobered by the threat, the first time she'd looked defeated since she'd entered the courtroom. "No," she said.

"Then, please," said Tracy, "describe for this courtroom the first time you and Mr. Silver had sex."

"It was Easter," said Robin, "just a couple of months after the concert."

The Gunslinger stepped out of the shadows with a gift-wrapped box in her hands. She gave it to Robin, then disappeared again. And, as she vanished, the room began to transform. Tracy knew this place all too well: the old footlocker and the strong scent of its cedar lining, the plastic bins full to the brim with Cabbage Patch Kids and Care Bears and Pound Puppies, the beat-up plaid couch with the thick wooden arm rests. It was the rec room of the Cape house, and it looked almost the same in 1995 as it did now.

"No one else was awake yet," said Robin. "And the first thing he said to me, when I gave him his present was—"

"Oh no, you're turning into the batty neighbor."

"What do you mean?" said Robin.

"You're confusing holidays," said Michael, "just like she does."

"How so?" said Robin.

"It's Easter," said Michael, "and you're giving me a present. Presents, as you know, are for Christmas."

"You're ridiculous," said Robin. "Just open it."

Michael sighed, then started in on the package's ribbons, its bow.

"Just out of curiosity," said Robin, "how is it that she's mixing things up?"

"You didn't see it?" said Michael.

"See what?" said Robin.

"Oh, Christ," said Michael. "Let me finish opening this and then I'll show you."

He finished opening the package and his face was all mirth and mischief as he pulled from it a plastic baby in a burlap swaddling cloth.

"Is this what I think it is?" said Michael.

"Yep," said Robin. "I stole it from her yard this morning."

Tracy had heard stories of this doll, of where it came from. The next door neighbor, Mrs. Doris Brown, before she passed away, had kept a nativity scene in her yard year round. But Michael, the family atheist, didn't buy that. Since the only time he saw it was at Easter, when he came down to visit, he swore up and down that the woman was just losing her marbles and mixing up her holidays.

Michael contemplated the baby. He paced with it, holding it by the feet and tapping its head against the palm of his free hand. Then, suddenly, he stopped and removed its swaddling cloth. He stared down at the naked doll, dumbfounded.

"No dick," he said.

"Excuse me?" said Robin.

Michael held the baby close to his face, inspecting its crotch.

"No dick," he repeated. "The son of God has no dick. Now I get it. Now I know why we're all so sexually frustrated."

Robin guffawed, then covered her mouth, looking toward the stairs, maybe to see if anyone was coming, if they'd woken anyone.

"I mean, shit," he said. "I knew they cut off the tip, but this is a bit much, don't you think? We are definitely not converting to Judaism."

Michael hoisted the baby high above his head and bellowed, "I have seen the loins of Jesus Christ, and they have shown me the light!"

Robin held a finger to her lips, trying to shush him, but she had the giggles now, and her attempt didn't last long; soon, she was doubled over with laughter.

Michael shook the baby at the window that overlooked Mrs. Brown's yard. "I don't know how many times we've told that woman that the nativity scene is for Christmas and not for Easter. But does she listen?" he said. "NO! I mean, Jesus! Is it too much to ask that, if you're going to put a tacky plastic sculpture on your lawn to celebrate your faith, you at least know what holiday it is? I'm no theology scholar, but this is pretty simple shit we're talking about here. I mean, why doesn't she put a plastic crucifixion scene on her lawn or something?"

"I don't think they make those," said Robin.

"I betcha," said Michael, "somebody could make a lot of money producing plastic crucifixion scenes."

He used the doll to illustrate his point, nodding and pointing as necessary. "See," he said, "you've got Jesus over here, and then you've got the two thieves over here and here. And of course we can't forget about Mary, with the cherry, and Mary Magdalene, and the Romans—"

"Stop it!" said Robin. "You're killing me."

Michael put the baby down. "I'm sorry," he said. "Thank you for my present."

"You're welcome," she said. "Now, sit. I've got something to tell you."

Michael sat on the floor of the rec room. He grabbed a raggedy old Cabbage Patch Kid and held onto it as he said, "I have a bad feeling about this."

Robin sat across from him and took hold of his hand, the Cabbage Patch Kid slumping in his lap now.

"I'm just going to come right out and say it," she said.

"OK," said Michael.

"Carl Jacobson," she said.

"The football player?"

"Just once," she said. "At a party. I was playing my guitar, and he was looking at me just the right way, and there was a lot of Schlitz involved, and—"

"Just once, meaning what?" said Michael. "I mean, you and I haven't even—"

"No, not that!" said Robin. "We just made out for a while."

Michael took his hands back, wrapped his arms around the Cabbage Patch Kid again. Then he reached out and grabbed a Pound Puppy for good measure. "Why did you tell me?" he asked.

"What do you mean?" she said. "I wanted to be honest with you. Isn't honesty what great relationships are built on?"

"Great relationships are built on kindness," said Michael, running the Kid's fat hand over the Puppy's mottled fur. "Consideration," he said.

"And me telling you wasn't kind?" she said. "That wasn't considerate?"

"No," he said. "I know who you are, Robin. I know *what* you are."

Now she seemed taken aback. She scowled a bit. "What am I?"

"A bonafide fucking rock star," said Michael. "Or as close to a rock star as a 17-year-old can get."

"And what does that mean?" said Robin.

"It means," said Michael, "that I knew about Carl, and about the other guys before him, but that I accepted that was part of the deal in being with you. I accepted it and ignored it. And you keeping quiet about your indiscretions aided that cause."

"So," she said, "you'd rather I didn't say anything?"

"Yes!" he said, hurling the toys back in their bins. "I'd rather you let me labor under the delusion that a pretty girl would ever be interested in me, could ever be satisfied by me and me alone."

High above, on her platform, Tracy looked out into the darkness, both to avoid looking at the awkward scene playing out before her and to see how the jury was reacting. But she couldn't see them at all. It was as if they had disappeared, as if maybe they weren't there after all.

Robin was on her knees now, stretching her limber body

toward Michael. She wrapped her arms around his shoulders as she said, "You do satisfy me."

He kissed her then, and she kissed him back. They made out with wild abandon as he pushed her backwards and got on top of her.

"Have you no decency?" shouted Tracy. "You're a married—"

But they weren't listening. And was he even the same person now, or was he, in fact, the version of himself from all those years before, the unmarried one?

Does it matter? asked a voice in her head.

Robin began to tug his pants off. Tracy caught sight of the slightest hint of her uncle's ass crack and that was it; she was done. She banged her gavel down three times on the broken sounding block, splintering it further.

"That's enough," said Tracy. "Guards!"

The Swordswoman and the Gunslinger tore out of the darkness, then tore Michael off of Robin, the Swordswoman yanking his pants back up as they did.

Robin stomped over to the Gunslinger and threw a haymaker, dropping the woman to the ground, but stumbling over herself in the process, falling flat on her face.

"Stand up," said Tracy. "All of you."

The Swordswoman grabbed hold of Robin and yanked her up, pulling her off to one side. The Gunslinger, wiping at her bleeding lip, grabbed hold of Michael.

"Ms. Gates," said Tracy, "I have one final question for you, before you're dismissed."

"Yes?" said Robin.

"When Mr. Silver emailed you on the evening of January 22, 1998 to end your relationship, to what did he attribute his decision to call things off?"

"He told me he couldn't understand why I hadn't told him about the drummer from Berklee," she said. "He wanted to know why he'd had to find out from his cousin. Or his cousin's husband. Or something."

"He couldn't understand why you kept the affair from him, even though he had specifically asked you to keep your affairs from him?"

"That's right," said Robin.

"So," said Tracy, "it would be accurate to describe Mr. Silver as a hypocrite, would it not?"

Robin rolled her eyes. "Since when is it a crime to contradict yourself? People change, sometimes from day to day. Hell, I've lived my entire life as a walking contradiction."

Tracy looked around as the rec room faded and the courtroom reappeared, and she found the jury whispering to each other, nodding their approval. *Yes*, they seemed to be saying. *Contradiction is good sometimes. Necessary even.* She was losing them. But they had to see. She had to make them. "But your life is over because of your own hypocrisy," she said. "Shot by a fan you spurned after writing an album of songs begging the masses to adore you." Tracy shook her head, trying to push aside the memory of the tearful, snotty mess she'd been on the day she heard the news. "Ms. Gates, do you wish the same fate for Mr. Silver?"

"No," said Robin.

"Neither do I," Tracy said, and suddenly the courtroom fell silent. The whispers stopped and the gawking commenced. Had she really just said that? Out loud? While trying to win this case? "We're not just here to protect women from him," she said, stumbling for what to say next. "We're also here to protect him from himself."

She banged the gavel down once more. "The witness is excused."

Robin gazed longingly at Michael. Then, with a firm nudge from the Swordswoman, she stepped out of the light, fading back into the darkness from whence she came.

e stared now at two of the more audacious members of the jury. The first was a brown-skinned woman—*not a redhead*, Tracy realized, surprised, having thought the jury was nothing but. She wore a purple bathing suit, the left side of it an inexplicable gash of fish-net, from just below her breast to just above her hip. She had blue hair, green sunglasses, and dangly gold earrings that reached all the way down to the purple choker that held the suit up and her enormous chest in.

Beside her sat a redhead, one of the many, in a white kimono with purple trim, a magenta corset beneath it that was half leather and half skull-patterned lace. She wore a pair of handcuffs on her left wrist, a purple rose and its thorns on the right, and she held matching Comedy and Tragedy masks in each hand. The right half of her face was covered by her hair and three mascara-lined tears rolled down her left cheek. Tracy stifled a laugh. The woman's big 80s hair—that was tragic. But the rest of her get-up, all the half-assed attempts at symbolism, that was almost funny.

Michael shook his head as the two jurors stared at him, their eyes narrowed, their lips pursed. "This is a joke," he said. "How much more of this is there? How long until this shit wears off?"

"This is no joke," said Tracy. "And it doesn't end until you admit your guilt and accept your—"

"Okay then," Michael said to the women he'd been eyeing. "I'm guilty."

"Of what?" said Tracy.

"I don't know," he said, turning to face her now. "You tell me!"

Tracy shook her head. He wasn't ready yet, but that wasn't a surprise. She knew he wouldn't be. She knew it would take the whole journey to get him there.

"I would like to move on now," she said, "to your relationship with Ms. Jennifer Worthing."

"Jenna?" said Michael. "Don't you mean Mrs. Jenna Silver? If you insist on being official—"

"She doesn't belong to you," said Tracy, "no matter what her driver's license says. She was born Jennifer Worthing and—"

"So she belongs to her father then?"

"Excuse me?" said Tracy.

"Worthing was her father's name, and he left when she was five. So, why not give her the name she chose, rather than the one she was saddled with by that good for nothing—"

The lights changed, without Tracy doing anything and without, it seemed, Michael doing anything either. Onto the stage— for it was a stage now, not the courtroom anymore, and not their stage but something bigger—danced someone, a woman, a woman who said, "How about the two of you quit your bitching and let's get on with this?"

It was Jenna and the story Tracy was about to see play out was legend. Michael fell to the floor at the sight of his wife dancing in as her younger self. From his pocket, he withdrew a tiny paintbrush.

Tracy said, "When you met Ms. Worthing—"

"This isn't when I met her," said Michael. "We'd been living in the same townhouse for over two years at this point."

"Okay then," said Tracy. "When you and Ms. Worthing began your relationsh—"

"Why don't you just shut up and watch?" he said.

Michael was working on the last corner of a 48-by-48 foot backdrop with the tiniest brush he owned, a 9/128" red sable that he normally reserved for painting ceramics. Behind him, only Jenna's lingering feet were left, shuffling and skittering across the floor. Try as he might to stop himself, he could not help but glance over his shoulder in between strokes. He could not help, he had told Tracy once, but stare at the girl to whom the feet belonged.

Through the accident of her DNA, Jenna Worthing was possessed of the same idyllic body the Greeks had sculpted two thousand years before. Statuesque, all hips, she was more woman than any girl he had ever known. She spun slowly in her tight black leotard, her arms reaching upward, those full, womanly hips thrust outward, and her head back, her auburn hair falling downward in a matted mess, away from her sweat-soaked brow, from that soft, girl-like face of hers, that face that was, as always, devoid of any of the embellishments—the rouge, the eyeliner, the lip gloss—that might have more fully given her the façade of a grown woman. Wisps of hair clung to each of her apple cheeks, and a heavy, wet lock of it was strewn across those petite lips of hers, which curved upwards at the corners in the devilish little grin that seemed her most cherished facial expression. When she lifted a leg off of the floor, he could see that her foot was dirty, blackened from dancing atop the rubber floor for most of this cold winter's day. He turned away from her once he realized that he'd been staring at the cracks between her toes, and he wondered what he'd been looking for. Some splotch of pure, innocent pink? Who knew? Michael tapped at the bulge in his right jeans pocket, where he kept his wallet, inside which there was still, undoubtedly, a photograph of Robin. Then he painted some more.

Jenna sat down beside him when she was done, legs stretched

out in front of her, arms stretched backward to support herself as she stretched. She smelled deliciously awful, her scent a funky potpourri of perspiration and peppermint patties, burnt rubber and Bolognese sauce.

"Nobody," she said, panting in between gulps from her liter of spring water, "is ever going to notice this."

"I will," he said.

"I admire your dedication," she said, laying her head on his shoulder, her labored breath hot against his neck, her hair clinging to his cheek.

"Me, too," he said. "I mean, I admire your dedication. Not mine."

"Thanks," she said. "I wish that it would start paying off. Y'know?"

"You're too harsh on yourself," said Michael.

She patted him on the shoulder as she stood to go. "Aren't we all?"

Michael watched her walk away. Her leotard was riding up in the back, her firm bottom glistening with sweat. Robin, Tracy knew, wouldn't have been caught dead in the same situation. And that was what Michael must have been thinking about: Robin, running around looking for a sweater to wrap around her waist, or walking backwards toward the door, trying not to stumble over her own feet.

Jenna paused at the stage's side door and looked back at him. "You want to walk back to the house together?"

"Yeah," he said. "Yeah."

The bitter December wind whipped at them as they trudged across campus through the freshly fallen snow.

Originally founded when Thomas Jefferson was in office, Kimball College sat atop a wooded hill high above the city of Haverhill. Down in the city, along the banks of the Merrimack River, there had once been a thriving shoe industry. Now, like much of the city, the factories sat boarded-up and crumbling. But up here on the hill, behind the brick and iron fence that surrounded the whole of the campus, there remained a happy, hippy community of bohemians and n'er-do-wells. In the midst of a quiet residential neighborhood, the campus' sprawling lawns served as something of a public park, where children rode their bikes and families walked their dogs and where, from September to May, the student body was like the circus come to town—a rainbow of world cultures, of hair colors, and of sexual deviances in this place that had been, for almost two centuries, nothing more than a coven for rich men's daughters.

It was, Tracy happened to know, one of Michael's favorite places on earth.

The front of the campus presented to bustling South Main Street, and to the rest of the world beyond it, the façade of academia, a trio of harmonious buildings built in the classical style, all Doric columns and red brick, each of them flanking the "sacred sod" of the front lawn, on which you were not to tread until your commencement.

But the rest of the campus, beginning with the modern-looking library, all windows and gray concrete, stood in stark contrast. It was the many faces of Kimball that Michael loved, however: so much history, and yet so much of the here and now.

As the story went, they had crossed half of the campus before his mind wandered back to the girl at his side. Jenna was so bundled up that only a sliver of her face was visible, just between where her purple wool hat ended and her thick green scarf began. Her enormous winter coat added so much bulk to her frame that she more resembled a middle linebacker than a prima ballerina.

He smirked behind his own scarf. She would have beaten him silly had he made that comparison out loud. She was not, she told people early and often, when discussions of her dancing came up, a ballerina. She danced modern, and though she'd never say it out loud, her eyes would always add, "and please don't make that mistake again."

She didn't have the body of a ballerina, she was quick to point out. Her shoulders were too broad, her bust too big, her hips far too wide. Her legs were long enough, sure, but her neck was too short. And her technique—well, that was a whole other story. Her turnout had always been poor, her flexibility was mediocre at best, she couldn't do pointe at all, and she had the worst feet in the entire company. Once, when they'd been sitting around the living room floor of their townhouse, she'd caught Michael flexing his foot and simply marveled at his form, his arches, the way his first three toes were almost all the same length. "I'd kill for your feet," she'd said.

But he'd always taken her criticisms of her body the same way others seemed to take his criticisms of his paintings—they were both too close to their art to have any kind of perspective on it. Her body, in his humble opinion, was quite alright. She was what his grandfather would have called a "substantial" woman, not nearly as substantial as Grammy, but certainly a "healthy young lady," a compliment Grampy could never have paid to Robin.

As they passed over the footbridge, Michael cast a sideways glance over the railing down at the icy pond. The first time he'd brought Robin up here, to show her around, he'd tried to convince her to come up to school here instead of down in Boston, at Berklee. She'd be the star of the program, rather than just another voice in a chorus, just another guitarist in a school full of them. And she'd smiled at that, in that way that she always did, like his mother did whenever his father said something stupid, a sort of "Yes, dear" smirk that was meant to end the conversation. But he, like his father, was never good at picking up on that particular brand of smile, at least not until reflecting on it later, and he'd asked her, as they'd walked over this same bridge: "Berklee doesn't have a pond in the middle of campus now, does it?" And she'd nodded along, saying "No, I guess not." But Berklee is where she went anyway.

He hadn't said anything after that, but he'd wanted to. And

what he would've said, what he said to her in his head, planning the conversation that he would have with her if the opportunity ever presented itself again, was, "Look around you! Listen! Breathe! There's no clutter here, no buildings all hunched together. There's no exhaust filling your lungs, just fresh air. There's no honking, no swearing at the guy in front of you because he doesn't know how to make a right turn on red—if you want to move fast here, there's plenty of room to go around. I'm peaceful here. I can hear myself think. I know who I am here. How could you love me and not love this place?"

"Has she fessed up yet?" Jenna asked him, her voice still muffled by her scarf.

They passed underneath the glow of the floodlights that hung alongside a dorm as Michael searched for an answer to her question.

"I suppose she wouldn't, would she?" Jenna added.

"Maybe the Runt didn't see what he thinks he saw. He and my cousin don't exactly have a happy marriage."

"I don't think he'd have even bothered to call you if he wasn't sure."

The patch of his scarf right in front of his mouth was wet with saliva, and it chafed against his lips as he said, "I suppose."

A cluster of townhouses loomed in front of them now, huddled around their snowy common lawn like so many vagrants around a flaming garbage can—unapologetically too close for comfort. Their house, the last one on the right, was dark. Their housemates must've been saving their energy for tomorrow's opening night party, for that was the way the rest of them, as non-artists, found a way to share in the whole event.

Michael scowled behind his scarf, recalling Robin's laughter upon first sight of these delightfully derelict buildings, at how they stuck out, even back here on the weirder, non-traditional side of campus. Yes, they were too angular, too seventies in their design. And yes, they were gradually sinking into the mucky New

England soil. But they were charming, nevertheless, and oh, how he'd hated Robin that night. He'd taken her right back to the car, driven her home, and promised himself he would never bring her back. But the memories haunted him still, enveloped him in their irksome embrace.

In fact, they so enveloped him that he didn't notice the snowball careening towards his head that evening until it was too late. It hit the side of his head with a splat, the wet and cold seeping right through his hat and into his ear. Jenna was running down the path in front of him, laughing hysterically. He reached down into a towering bank and hurled a clump of snow at her, taking no time to ball it up, but she was out of range, already at their doorstep with her key in hand.

"What do you think I should do?" he asked her as they sat at the dining room table, sipping from mugs of steaming hot chocolate, their coats and scarves and hats draped over the other chairs.

"I've told you," she said, picking at the dried paint that covered his hands and forearms, piling up the flakes on the table in a neat stack. "You should dump her so that you and I can finally, you know, get it over with."

Michael winced as she plucked a huge chunk from his wrist, a clump of hair coming along with it.

"Sorry," she said, frowning for a moment before going back to work.

"What about your boyfriend?" he asked her.

She sighed, rubbing the edge of her thumbnail along a particularly stubborn piece of paint.

Michael ran his free hand along the top of his head, trying to smooth out the hair he could feel sprouting outward in a dozen different directions. He chuckled. "I love how you put it—we need to 'get it over with.'"

She kicked him lightly underneath the table. "I'm not the only one who thinks so."

He grabbed hold of her foot before she could steal it back.

When he began to knead at her naked arch with his thumb, she let go of the hand she'd been holding and leaned back in her chair, unclenching.

She moaned, "Mmm. That is sooooo nice..."

Michael shook his head and groaned, "Damn."

"You think too much," she said, flexing her foot in his hand as he stopped rubbing.

"You know what," he said. "I do. I do think too much. But never about the important things. At least not until lately. Now I can't stop thinking about all the stupid stuff she's put me through."

"Like her going and cheating on you," Jenna said, pulling her foot back from him.

"Like her going and cheating on me," Michael said, nodding.

Jenna leaned over the table and smiled at him. "Listen, could you maybe drop her for tonight?" And then, pausing for a moment, she added, "Or maybe for the rest of your life."

He picked up his hot chocolate and sipped from it.

"She was high school and now it's college. I went through the same thing." She held her mug up to her lips and tilted her head back, then set it down on the table, a frown on her face. She'd begun to rub a foot up under the cuff of his jeans, along his calf. "We've wasted too much of our time here," she said, picking up her mug again and tipping it upside down. "Everyone in this house came to college with a significant other, but they all came to their senses a long time ago. Now it's time for us to see the lights."

"You mean, 'the light,' singular, right?"

"Whatever," she said, reaching across the table for his mug, then sipping from it.

Michael laughed. "I just can't believe that a girl like you, a girl so talented, so beauti—"

"Oh, stop it," she said, handing him back his mug, her foot disappearing from his leg. "You're taking me out of the mood."

"You're the only girl I know who gets turned off by compliments about her appearance."

"It's not that," she said. "It's that I get annoyed when you don't give yourself enough credit. You do it with me. You do it with your art." She paused, seeming to consider whether she should really say what she wanted to say next and then, said, "You do it with everything."

"Point taken," he said. "And I guess... baseball teams do carry a personal masseuse, so, even though I wouldn't be on a team in your league, so to speak, I could conceivably become an employee of the league."

She chuckled at him. "You need to learn when to shut up."

"It's genetic."

Jenna stood and gathered up her things. "I'm going upstairs," she said. "Kate is gone for the night. So..." She paused and smiled. "Good night."

"G'night," he said, waving a little wave.

He watched her ascend the stairs until she'd rounded the corner to her room, then looked down the flight of stairs that led to his own bedroom. He tapped at his wallet again, and then pulled it out. He leafed through the photos he kept inside, past his cousin Matt, his sister Ashley, past Veronica and Tracy, past the miniature copy of the poem "Footprints" that his mother had bought for him after Grampy's funeral. The last picture was of Michael and Robin, from senior year, up on stage at the talent show, singing into the same microphone. They had sounded perfect, or so the stories went, so perfect as they sang, in harmony, "You can go your own way." He ran his fingers along the edges of her face, then closed his wallet and put it away.

And this was where Michael broke the fourth wall. Without looking at Tracy, he said, "This is the moment you've been working me up to, isn't it?"

"Yes," said Tracy.

"And are you going to let me have it?"

"Of course," said Tracy. "You need to have this moment. Or else the rest of it won't hurt as much."

Michael stood, then climbed the stairs.

Jenna took her time in answering his knock. She was wearing a longish t-shirt that fell down to her hips. "Are you sure?" she asked him. "Because I don't want to force you."

"I'm sure," he said.

She opened the door wider, took him by the hand, and pulled him in.

Up on the judge's bench, as all light went out, Tracy banged her gavel down three times. Below, torches in hand, the Gunslinger and Swordswoman stood waiting.

Tracy looked off in the direction where the ghost of Jenna's door still blurred her vision. She closed her eyes, pinched the bridge of her nose, hoping to regain her bearings, her focus and purpose. But, in the dark of her own mind, she could now hear the faintest sounds of lovemaking in the distance.

No, she thought. *Fucking! It's fucking. What they're doing is cheating, not love. He doesn't even know how to—*

She opened her eyes, focused on the guards. "We will adjourn for a brief recess," she told the two of them, "I need a moment."

❧ 8 ❧

AN INTERLUDE

U p in the house and unaware of what was going down in her barn, Veronica dreamed herself and her wife into the bed of Christy Turlington. They were tangled together under a thin white sheet, underneath the canopy of an enormous four-poster, a gentle breeze playing with the curtains by the window and the curtains of the bed. Veronica had an arm around each woman, their heads resting on her chest, their foreheads nearly touching but not quite. And while Veronica ran her fingers through their hair, they watched *Pretty Woman* on a thirteen-inch TV with a VCR built into the bottom of it. It was perched precariously on the end of the bed and threatened to topple off the pillowed top of the mattress at any moment. Only the feet of Christy and Desiree held it in place.

Why is the TV so small? Veronica wondered. *Surely a supermodel can afford something grander than this. And a VCR in 2011?*

That was when she woke, the logic of the dream crumbling like a leaning tower of Jenga blocks that you've stared at for too long, the mash-up of sexual fantasy and old childhood memory giving her a shiver that woke her from her slumber. She turned from her side to see if Desiree was awake, if there was someone she could share this pleasant but curious vision with, but Des wasn't in bed.

Veronica sat up, rubbing at her eyes, and found her wife perched in the rocking chair by the window, staring out the old dormer and into the night. By the light of the moon, Veronica could see that Des was biting her thumb.

"What?" said Veronica.

"That space bastard," she said, "he killed my pine."

Space bastard? thought Veronica. Was she still dreaming, she wondered.

"*Back to the Future*," Desiree explained. "When Marty first ends up in 1955 and he runs over one of Old Man Peabody's saplings in the DeLorean."

Veronica was confused. "There's a DeLorean out there?" she asked, scooting out of bed. "And a space bastard?" she asked as she knelt down behind Desiree and wrapped her arms around her.

"Tracy's date," said Desiree, pointing at a now-disheveled hedgerow near the edge of their property. "He hit it as he peeled out of here."

Veronica nuzzled her wife's neck, then her ear. "Baby," she said, "how long have you been up?"

Desiree took hold of one of Veronica's hands and brought it to her lips. Then she sighed and leaned into her wife's embrace. "Too long," she said.

"And what did you see?" asked Veronica.

"The kids parking their car down by the beach," she began, "then them creeping up into the barn."

"Tana and Tori were with her?" asked Veronica.

Desiree nodded.

"I love those girls," said Veronica. "Reminds me of us," she said, nipping at Des' earlobe, "when we were their age."

"A long time ago," said Desiree. "In a galaxy far, far away."

Veronica nudged her wife. "So, what happened next, Uatu?"

"Uatu?" said Desiree.

"The Watcher," Veronica explained. "From the comic books? He's a space bastard with a big head," she said. "He watches things."

Desiree smiled and kissed Veronica's hand again. With her eyes still fixed on the window, she continued. "The date, he ran back to his car for something. But then everything was quiet for a couple of hours. By the time I heard the front door creak open downstairs, the porch steps groaning under someone's weight, I was about to nod off. I looked down and saw that it was Michael, headphones in, going for a stroll. And where do you think he strolled to?"

"Shut up," said Veronica, slapping Des on the shoulder.

"Yep," said Desiree. "He went straight for the barn. Couple minutes later, Tana, Tori, and the date come racing out of there— the date tripping over his half-buckled jeans, I might add—and they all make for the car."

"And Michael and Trace," said Veronica, pointing toward the barn, "they've been in there ever since?"

Desiree nodded.

"How long?" said Veronica.

"A while," said Desiree. "Just before you woke up, I was thinking of going down there."

Veronica pulled out of their embrace and shimmied on her knees until she'd rounded the chair and was facing Des. "You can't do that," she told her wife. "You need to let them work it out on their own."

"But you didn't see how mad she was at him," said Desiree, taking Veronica's face into her hands. "Not the half of it. I caught her upstairs after the show last night and she... she's really pissed, Vern. I don't know why exactly, but—"

"It's between them," said Veronica, taking hold of Desiree's hands and lacing their fingers together. "Father and daughter stuff," she said.

"He's not her father," said Desiree.

"He's the closest thing she has to one," said Veronica.

"But," Desiree began, but whatever she was about to say was cut off by the sound of a door slamming open outside.

Veronica spun on the spot as Desiree leaned forward, and the two of them peered out the dormer window to see what was happening. As they did, Tracy came storming out of the barn in a huff. Hands on her hips, she paced the length of the barn as they watched.

"That's a cute top she's wearing," said Veronica. "A hand-me-down from you?"

Desiree nodded, frowning. "It's on backwards."

Down below, as if she'd heard them, Tracy quit her pacing and stared up at the window for a moment. Veronica thought to duck, but Tracy was moving again just as quickly as she'd come to a halt. She shook her head and looked to be mumbling something to herself.

"You think she saw us?" said Veronica.

"I think we should go down there," said Desiree. "That's what I think. Or maybe wake Jenna and send her out, if what you're worried about is us being overbearing."

"She's 18," said Veronica, looking back at Des over her shoulder. "This is the part of the story where she figures things out on her own."

"Is it?" said Desiree. "And if it is, then why is it? Because that's what you had to do?"

Veronica grunted, then said, "I had to figure things out on my own long before she did."

Desiree squeezed Veronica's shoulders. "Right," she said, "but do you want to be your dad?"

Veronica spun around again. She narrowed her eyes and stared up into Desiree's face, determined to find an answer there, a compromise. But she couldn't. So, instead, she held out one open palm before her and then set a closed fist atop it.

"What are you doing?" said Desiree.

"Rock, paper, scissors," said Veronica. "No fairer way to decide," she said.

"Parenting by Roshambo?" said Desiree, shaking her head and smirking despite herself.

"Yep," said Veronica, nodding at her outstretched hands.

"I guess this is what happily ever after looks like," said Desiree, mirroring Veronica's hands now and getting ready to duel. "Dumb and so saccharine it'll rot our goddamn teeth straight out of our increasingly empty heads."

"You ask me," said Veronica, "the Brothers Grimm—"

"I don't think people lived happily ever after in their versions," said Desiree. "Mostly I think they had their eyes put out by ravens, or else they sawed off their own toes to win the love of aloof princes."

"You knew what I meant," said Veronica. "The fairy tale people," she said, "I think they end things too early. I think it's possible, however unlikely, that happily ever after could be a lot more interesting than it lets on."

"Fine," said Desiree, shaking her head and rolling her eyes. "Are you ready?"

Veronica nodded. Then, together, tapping fists against open palms on each beat, they said, "Rock, paper, scissors." But before they could say "shoot," the barn door slammed shut down below. Veronica and Desiree turned from each other and cast their gazes out of the window again, but Tracy had gone back inside.

"Come back to bed," said Veronica.

"Shoot," said Desiree, shaping her index and middle fingers into a pair of scissors and waiting for Veronica's response.

Paper or rock, Veronica had to decide. She looked into her wife's eyes, as she always did, for the answer.

A s she stormed back into the courtroom, it was Tracy's nose that stopped her in her tracks.

It was filled, all at once, with the smells of plumeria and pineapple, of sunblock and aloe vera, of a pig roasting on a spit.

Then there was sound: rain pounding down on the roof overhead, rain sizzling as it hit the hot pork, the slap of bare feet racing across cold stone. And, somewhere beyond all that, waves crashing on a not-so-distant shore.

Finally, there was light and a whole lot of it. Tracy blinked her eyes against the burst of color, rubbing them until they adjusted. The room she found herself looming above now was all wicker and white linen, open to the elements on three sides, a collection of Polynesian art on the fourth. Michael's own painting of Pele was the centerpiece, a fierce portrait of the goddess emerging from a lava flow to confront a trio of suit-clad men breaking ground where they shouldn't have been.

She looked around for some sign of Michael, who was the mastermind behind all this. His ability to bend the world to his liking was frightening. Her mother hadn't been able to do this, at least not this well, at least not as far as Tracy knew. They were already in Hawaii, and they weren't meant to be there yet. Michael was in control, and Tracy didn't like that one bit. She remembered her mother's dream about the Salesman, how frightened Veronica said he'd been when she had taken control when she wasn't supposed to. It was happening to Tracy now. But she couldn't let it. She had to find a way to turn things around.

A board game sat open, in mid-play, on the dining table. It was Risk, if Tracy was right, a game of military strategy and world domination. She wondered at the significance, beyond the name of course, which was surely meant to refute her claim that Michael didn't make choices in his life.

"Mr. Silver!" she shouted, hoping her voice would draw him out. "What is the meaning of—"

"I'm defending myself," he shouted back, as he strode into the room. He looked confident, victorious even.

Tracy said, "The prosecution hasn't finished its—"

"Whatever rules this farce might have had," said Michael, "you broke them first!" He waved at someone in the hallway and then, through the doorway, walked Jenna and Veronica. Veronica strummed a happy tune on the ukulele and they both sang along. Then they seated themselves and looked at their cards, examined their positions on the board.

Tracy threaded her fingers together and pushed her thumbs together, trying to keep her composure. This looked good. This looked like he had something. She breathed, then said, "You try this court's patience, Mr. Silver. But, given how unlikely it is that your evidence will sway us, we'll allow it. Would you care to set the scene?"

"It was the summer of 2002," said Michael, "a little over a year after Jenna and I were married. We'd moved to Hawaii after honeymooning there and your mothers decided to pay us a visit."

"And where was I?" said Tracy.

Michael sat at the table, picked up a pair of six-sided dice. "Back in Massachusetts," he said, "with your father."

"He's not my—"

"Oh," said Michael, "that sniveling little coward is your father, alright. The family resemblance has never been clearer than it is right now."

Tracy banged down her gavel in anger just as Michael rolled the dice. That was when the ladies at the table started speaking.

"How big are the needles?" said Jenna.

"Wait!" said Michael. "There are needles?"

"Yes," said Veronica. "There are needles. Two different kinds, actually. Subcutaneous and intramuscular."

"And which kind is it that Desiree is on now?" said Jenna.

"Intramuscular," said Veronica.

"Intramuscular?" said Michael. "As in inside the muscle?"

Veronica smirked. "Yep."

"Egads," said Michael.

"What are you squirming about?" said Jenna. "You're not the one who'd be getting the shots."

"Yeah," he said, "but I'm the one who'd be administering them."

"You can't do them yourself?" said Jenna.

Veronica shook her head. "Desiree did the subcutaneous ones herself, from time to time. But not the intramuscular. Too much contorting."

Michael raised an eyebrow. "Where do you have to stick them?"

Veronica said, "The upper outer quadrant of a buttock."

"Ouch," said Michael, rubbing his own ass.

"Oh, quit your worrying," said Jenna. "I've survived being married to you for a year. I know how to deal with a pain in the ass."

Tracy laughed, in spite of herself. Michael and Jenna's banter had always been her favorite part of having them around. But something was gnawing at her, as the conversation continued: How had she not known about this? How had her mothers kept it all a secret?

"There was no other way for her to get pregnant?" said Michael.

"There were a few," said Veronica. "But, seeing as she didn't want to reenact that Heart song—"

"Which Heart song?" said Jenna.

Veronica smiled and Michael groaned, their typical reactions to Jenna's lack of pop culture knowledge. Veronica illuminated her. "'All I Wanna Do Is Make Love To You,'" she said.

"Which one is that?" said Jenna.

Michael explained: "The one where she picks up a dude on the side of the road for the express purpose of knocking herself up."

"Oh," said Jenna.

"Yeah," said Veronica. "So, that was out. We did try artificial insemination, but it didn't take."

"Didn't take?" said Jenna. "You mean, she had a—"

"Yep," said Veronica.

Jenna grabbed hold of Veronica's hand. Up on the bench, Tracy wished she could do the same. She braced her upper lip against her lower, thinking of what her mothers had lost, of who. A face came to mind, a little old man's wrinkled, toothless face, but on a cherub's soft pink body. She squeezed her eyes shut.

"I'm sorry," said Jenna.

"Water under the bridge," said Veronica, as Tracy opened her eyes again. Veronica addressed the game, waving a hand over the board. "Whose turn is it?"

"Mine," said Michael.

Veronica said, "Then what's your move, Professor?"

"Shh!" said Michael. "Don't jinx it. I haven't graduated the program yet. And, even if I do, I'm not sure I would want to be a profes—"

"Waitaminute," said Veronica. "You haven't wowed them yet with your thesis on those perverted pin-ups?"

Michael's thesis! It was one of Tracy's favorite texts, both the spiral-bound review copy he gave her the day after he successfully defended his dissertation, as well as the version that the University Press of New England published a few years after that. The premise, as famous now in the art world as it had been for years in their family, was that Nick Gold, a pin-up artist and comic book penciller from the 1940s, was actually an alias of Michael's Great Aunt Dottie. She was a lesbian trying to break into a male-dominated industry, and Michael posited that it was only because of her male pseudonym that her drawings of half-naked women were as popular as they were. Michael said that, if readers knew it was a woman drawing the stuff they were jerking off to, it never would have worked.

"Oh, please don't get him started," Jenna begged Veronica. "Can we just play?"

"Of course," said Veronica. "What's your play, Prof?"

Michael winced at the nickname, just as Veronica might wince if the name of the Scottish Play were mentioned within fifty feet of the barn. Then, he said, "I'm invading Camel Crap."

"Camel what?" said Jenna.

"Kamchatka," said Veronica. "It was the nickname our fathers had for Kamchatka."

"But," said Jenna, "Kamchatka doesn't sound anything like—"

Together, Michael and Veronica said, "We know."

"Did you roll?" said Veronica.

"Sure did," said Michael. "Beat that, cuz."

Veronica picked up the dice and rolled. Then she smiled as Michael jolted back away from the table.

"Damn!" he said. "I never win, dude. Never."

Veronica plucked several pieces off of the game board tile representing Alaska and deposited them back into the game's box. "And," she said, "the mighty army of Camel Crap beats back the pitiful Alaskan hordes once again."

As Jenna picked up the dice to roll, Desiree crept into the room, lingering in the doorway. When the rest of them turned to face her, she manufactured a smile, but the craftsmanship was shoddy and Veronica saw right through the façade. Up on the bench, Tracy did too.

"Hi," said Desiree.

Veronica rose from the table and made her way across the room. "What happened?" she said.

"What do you mean?" said Desiree. "Nothing—"

"Des," said Veronica.

"We can talk about it later," said Desiree, taking a step toward the table.

Jenna rose, pushed her seat back, and tapped Michael on the shoulder. She said, "We can give you guys some privacy."

"No," said Desiree. "No, I don't want to... Not right now."

"Is it the baby?" said Michael.

Tracy wanted to leap down and smack him, to pummel him with her fists until he was weeping on the floor, weeping the way she wanted to weep now. First, he had to show her this in the first place, another piece of him she didn't want. Then, he had to say that, to ask that stupid question, in that stupid way. She wanted to rip at his neck until she could pull his larynx out of there, then to stomp on his voice right in front of him, until all the words he had left to say were nothing but a bloody mess on his tile floor.

Desiree broke down and began to cry into the crook of Veronica's shoulder. Veronica held Des tight, held her own tears back.

"It's not because you flew," said Michael, "is it?"

"Michael!" said Jenna. "Let's go."

Now Michael began to tear up. He turned to Jenna, said, "I'm the one who convinced them to fly out here."

"It's not because we flew," said Veronica, guiding Desiree out of the room. "It's not your fault."

Jenna turned on Michael. She said everything Tracy wanted to say, which was the only thing keeping Tracy where she was. "It has nothing to do with you," said Jenna. "How dare you inject yourself into—"

"Did you see how crushed she looked?" said Michael. "If there's anything I could have done, Jenna. If—"

"There's nothing you could have done," said Jenna. "It has nothing to do with you."

"Why," said Michael, "are you so mad at me for caring?"

Jenna stalked away from him. She stood by edge of the lanai and held a hand out into the rain. Then she brought that hand to her forehead, used it so push her hair back, away from her face. She closed her eyes, breathed.

Tracy admired this woman so much, pitied her. The things she put up with, even from perfect, sensitive, gentlemanly Michael.

"I'm not mad at you for caring," said Jenna. "I'm mad because you're falling apart, and it isn't even your baby."

"Yeah," said Michael. "But it's my cousin's, and—"

"Yes," she said. "It was your cousin's. And what would happen if it were yours?"

Michael said he didn't understand.

"Michael," said Jenna, "you're a sensitive soul. I get that. I love that about you. But in this situation, if we're going to go through this, one of us needs to be strong. And I'm telling you right now, it can't always be me."

"But we know this wouldn't happen to us," said Michael, standing, going to her. "I mean, the women in your family pop out babies just by thinking about it. I'm the one with the problem in our equation."

"So," said Michael, reaching for her hand, "if all we need is to give my guys a little guidance, then—"

"Then it could still fail," said Jenna, pulling her hand away, not yet ready to give it. "It could still fail. And what happens then? Do you turn into a blubbering mess when I need you the most?"

Michael walked away from her, went to the wall, and plucked the statue of Haumea off of the shelf. *Of course he did*, thought Tracy. *The fertility goddess, the most obvious prop in the room.*

"You want kids," he said to Jenna, turning to face her again, clutching the statue to his chest. "Don't you?"

"Yes," said Jenna.

"Then why are we even having this discussion? Why are we pretending like not doing the IVF is an option?"

"Because," said Jenna. "It is an option."

"It's not!" said Michael. "You want kids. End of story. We have to do this."

"No," said Jenna. "We don't. If you can't handle it—"

"I can handle it!" said Michael, setting Haumea back on her shelf. "Find me one of those needles," he said, heading back to the table, grabbing the strap of Veronica's pocket book. "I'll show you. I'm not gonna pass out at the sight of—"

"OK," said Jenna, "you'll get over your fear of needles. But what about everything else?"

"What else?" said Michael.

Jenna sat back down at the table. She said nothing for a moment, began to clear the board of the game's pieces. Then, she looked at him. She said, "What about the fact that you might not have a choice about that theoretical professorship Veronica was teasing you about? One of us is going to have to get a job, the nine-to-five kind, the kind with health insurance attached."

"Oh, man," said Michael, "you know I hate talking about that shit. I mean, why do we need health insurance? Plenty of people—"

Jenna sighed, leaning back in her chair. She rubbed at her temples, probably trying to keep her head from imploding under the sheer weight of his idiocy, his naïveté. "Oh, Michael," she said. "Jesus Christ! Have you read any of the emails Veronica has sent us, looked at any of the websites?"

"We're not going to be able to afford it without insurance?"

"No," said Jenna, "we're not."

Michael ducked his head, something finally sinking into it. "I didn't realize that," he said.

"There's a lot you didn't realize, apparently."

"But I want kids," he said. "I do."

"I know you do," she said, reaching for his hand, squeezing it. "We all want a lot of things in life. But there are only some wants that we actually get."

He turned away from her, pulled away from her grip, but she held on.

"Maybe," he said, "you should go out and make like that Heart song then? Find a dude by the side of the road and—"

Jenna stood, pulled at his hand, and spun him around. "I don't want a dude by the side of the road," she said.

Michael leaned his forehead against hers. "But the one thing I can't give you," he said, quoting the song, "is the one little thing that he can."

"Yeah," said Jenna, "but all I want to do is make love to you, you idiot. You, not someone else."

Tracy looked down on them for a moment, frozen there in their dining room. It had been nearly nine years since this moment, and she'd never heard of it. So many things about it stunned her, kept her tongue in her mouth and her mind inside itself, but the thing that shocked her most was that Michael had managed to keep something secret, that there was something she hadn't uncovered in all the digging she'd done.

"I didn't know," she said, as she tapped her gavel against the podium and washed the courtroom in darkness once again.

Michael stepped back into his pool of light. He stared up at her. "You think I can't make decisions?" he said. "Well, there you go: the toughest decision I've ever made."

"Except that you didn't make it," said Tracy. "Your wife did."

He shook his head, stomped from one edge of the circle to

the other. "We made the decision together," he said. "That's how marriage works, you little—"

Tracy banged the gavel down. From the darkness on either side of Michael came the guards, each brandishing their weapon of choice.

"One more insult," said Tracy, "and I'll find you in contempt of court."

"I have nothing but contempt for this court!" shouted Michael. As he did, something rather odd happened, something he seemed to notice almost as quickly as she did. The darkness around him flashed, for the briefest of moments, to a scene from some cartoon. There was a robot, a car rearranged to look like a man, delivering the same line Michael had just spoken. The first robot, all orange and gold, the hot head, stood beside another robot, all blue and gray, who was complaining about not being to transform. Above them, an egg-shaped robot with many faces was passing judgement. Below them, a school of robot sharks circled in a yellow-green pool.

Michael raised an eyebrow as the image faded away, then closed his eyes tight, as if in concentration, as if maybe trying to conjure another image.

Out of the darkness came the briefest flashes of other court-rooms, other scenes. There was a battle-hardened Marine losing his shit on the stand while being grilled by a punk-ass Navy lawyer, a Spartan king kicking a Persian messenger into a vast pit upon his warrior queen passing judgement, a city kid using the Bible to convince a small town's council members to let him and his friends dance, a bespectacled district attorney playing a horri-fying film of an assassination over and over again to make a point.

This was getting out of hand. Michael knew. He knew now that he wielded as much power as she did. "I am trying to help you," she called out to him, hoping to break his concentration, to get a reaction out of him, any reaction. "I'm trying to reform you."

Michael's eyes shot open. The visions stopped and the darkness returned. "Reform me!?" he said. "There's nothing wrong with me! Have you seen any of these women complaining about who I am or how I treated them? You're the one with the complaint. So, out with it! Quit dancing around the fucking subject and tell me what I did to you."

Good, she thought. *Crisis averted.* She spoke. "I will get there when I'm good and ready," she said. "But first, one more thing."

It was time, she knew, for the big guns. She shuffled through the papers in front of her. From the stack, she pulled a multi-page document that looked like it had been torn apart and taped back together again.

"Do you know what this is?" Tracy asked him.

"I have no idea," said Michael. The gulp of air he took after he said it said otherwise.

"It is a print-out," said Tracy, "of a message you composed. Composed, but never sent."

"Where did you get that?" said Michael.

She had hacked his email account, easy enough to do when his idea of a password was his wife's initials and her date of birth.

"I was hurt when I wrote that," he said. "Things were rough."

"But you don't deny writing it?" she said.

"I don't even remember what I wrote," he said. "But I never sent it. I made a *choice* not to."

"You don't remember what you wrote?" said Tracy.

"I don't," said Michael, though the color of his skin was growing paler and paler.

"Well then," said Tracy, "let me remind you."

⁂ 10 ⁂

Carrie,

The photo is of you, you sitting on a rock on the beach we all drove to on the final afternoon of the Boston conference. It was hot, and we'd known we were headed for the ocean, but none of us had thought to wear shorts (or maybe we had packed none). The cuffs of your jeans are wet, your feet are bare, and you're leaning back, supported by your hands, your ring finger not yet naked. You don't see me taking the picture. I didn't remember taking it until now.

I have a computer now which organizes my photos for me, which searches long forgotten corners of my hard drive, pushes aside digital cobwebs, and pulls eight-legged memories into the light. The program that does this is connected to a World Wide Web where I can set these spiders free, if I choose, and see if they are squashed as pests or made pets by button-clicking arachnophiles.

Oh, what a terrible metaphor. How is it that I, with paragraphs like that, was a prize winner, and you, with your ability to turn a phrase, were but the lowly administrator?

My mouse cursor hovers above an upload button as I wonder about you and the baby in your belly, about my wife and the womb I've left barren, about what could have been different, what would still be the same. If only. If.

This program sorts photos by location too, and my first discovery gets me wondering if there's more evidence of what happened in those six cities, over the course of those six years. So, instead of saying the hell with it, instead of clicking the button and seeing what happens, I go exploring.

⚜

WE MET IN NEW ORLEANS, on Bourbon Street, the year before the flood. I'd been nursing Diet Cokes and listening to the house band at a little joint called Fritzel's, way down past the strip clubs and the sports bars. My colleagues, who'd been hammered since halfway through that evening's banquet and keynote address, and who hadn't heard a damned note of the music since we'd arrived, had finally driven me off. I hadn't gotten out much since the conference started on Friday afternoon, and now that I'd presented my paper and the nerves were gone, I'd been hoping to get a taste of the real N'awlins before flying home. That they'd ruined that for me, as they'd ruined so much else for me that weekend, with their shoddy second-rate scholarship during the conference and their meandering, misogynistic anecdotes after hours, that was unforgivable.

So, I left Fritzel's and started back down Bourbon, headed in the direction of the Monteleone, where we were all staying. I made my way past Big Daddy's, where a pair of fishnet-clad mannequin's legs swung in and out of a window; past a karaoke club where some unseen gentleman screeched his best impression of Jon Bon Jovi; and past a sports bar where the New England Patriots, my hometown team, were on the TVs, beating up on the Buffalo Bills. But, despite the fact that a visit to a kitschy strip club probably would've sated my desire to see the real New Orleans just as much as listening to some European jazz, despite the fact that "Living on a Prayer" tops my list of guilty pleasure songs, and despite the fact that I hadn't missed a Pats game since they played in a blizzard three years before, I did not stop. The night was ruined. It was irreparable.

And then I spotted you, the prim and proper administrator of our young organization, your hair down both literally and figuratively, walking out of the Gold Club, your face flush, your body too, skin all aglow from your plunging neckline to your sweating forehead. There was an immense smile spreading across your face, and it only spread wider as you saw me draw near.

"Having fun?" you said.

"Trying," I said.

You shook a thumb over your shoulder, back at the club. "I was just leaving, but if you want to go back in, I'll buy you a dance."

"I doubt my wife would approve."

You laughed. "My husband would shit himself. But that's the whole point. Why else do we go to conferences?"

"The scholarship, I would hope."

Even me, at my most morose, could not bring you down. You shook your head at me. "You headed back to the hotel?" you asked.

I nodded. "I'd been hoping to catch some jazz, but—"

"You try Fritzel's?"

"Yes," I said. "I remembered your suggestion. Trouble is, so did everyone else."

"Yeah," you said. "That's the trouble with conferences. You have to discover something early, before all of your friends ruin it."

"I wouldn't call them friends," I said. "At least not at this point."

"A wise man," you said. "But, anyway, about the jazz: follow me!"

You grabbed me by the arm and led me off, past the hotel, down one side street after the other, until we found ourselves across the street from a run down sandwich place that was just closing up shop, the sign advertising authentic Po-Boys flickering from bright white to dull gray. The lights went out and then, just as they did, a mournful horn sounded out from inside. You laid your head on my shoulder as we eavesdropped on what seemed to me like a very private lament. I began to ask you if maybe we shouldn't feel wrong about this, but you shushed me before I was through.

"You don't blow like that if you don't want to be heard," you told me later.

৩৵৪

IN BOSTON THE NEXT YEAR, I sat with you in the dark, at the registration desk, as you ate the dinner you'd been too nervous to touch during the banquet. The keynote, given by the eldest scholar of our bunch, had descended, during the Q&A, into a drunken argument between the group's two belligerent factions. You cut into your re-heated steak with murder in your eyes, and as your meat spilled its juices onto the gleaming white plate, I imagined you imagining your knife slicing through the necks of those argumentative assholes.

"At least it's over," I said.

"It shouldn't have even started," you said. "The way these people can make anything political. Christ!"

"This stuff matters to us," I said. "And when something matters to you this much, and you get together with folks who care about it just as much as you do, arguments are bound to—"

"It's just a bunch of stories!" you shouted. You blanched as you looked around, searching the hall to see if anyone else had heard you. Then you set down your fork and knife, dabbed at your lips with your napkin, and whispered, "All they're arguing about are words and pictures on a goddamned page. The little things, the stupid things—that's all anyone ever argues about."

I didn't know what to say. You were right, of course. But I couldn't say that out loud, and I had to stop even thinking it before I drove myself nuts with the thought. So, I said, "You want to go to the beach tomorrow and cool off after everything's wrapped up."

You smiled. "Sure," you said. "That'd be nice."

࿓

IN SAN FRANCISCO, you didn't want to leave the hotel, but nobody could figure out why. This was your city, after all, and there was an expectation—and not an unreasonable one—that you would be our guide. But you shunted those duties off to an intern and stayed indoors, dashing between sessions, checking in on the volunteers manning the registration desk, disappearing into your room for hours on end.

It was before dawn on the last day that you collected me from my room and decided to spill the beans. We walked out of the Sir Francis Drake, away from Union Square, and headed north on Powell. Up hills we went, and down them, and up them again. For the most part, you said nothing, the only sounds you made the grunts you directed at the billboards hanging overhead.

It was only once we reached Fisherman's Wharf, when you'd grunted for the seventh time, that I commented on this, that I asked you what was wrong.

"They're everywhere," you said.

"Billboards?"

"Those billboards," you said, pointing.

The sign in question was one of dozens I had seen and immediately forgotten about over the past year, not just there in San

Francisco, but back home as well. It advertised a ubiquitous gadget of the moment with a dancing silhouette set against a pastel backdrop. I had no idea why the signs bothered you so—these things were so omnipresent now that they just blended in with the scenery for most of us—but bother you they did. I was about to ask when you spoke up again.

"He makes those things," you said. "My husband."

"Your husband?"

"Yes," you said. "Or, well, my ex... or soon-to-be... Or, well..."

"Oh," I said. "And these billboards, they're the reason you haven't gone out?"

"Do you notice what's wrong with them?"

I turned my critic's eye to the billboard, trying to spot something.

"Her ribcage," you said. "She's been Photoshopped, and her ribcage is slightly out of proportion. Slightly," you said again.

"I know Photoshop," I said, squinting. "Like, I *know* Photoshop. But I don't see it.

"No one does," you said. "No one except him. And now me. He made me stare at it until I couldn't help but notice it, until it was all I noticed."

"The little things," I said.

"The stupid things," you said, pushing the palm of your hand into the corner of your eye, wiping away something you didn't want me to see. "Anyway," you said. "Want to go see the Golden Gate?"

☙❦❧

IN CHICAGO, we shared a deep-dish pizza the night you told me that it was finally over, that the papers had come through and you were officially a "free" woman. But you didn't want to talk about it. You were ready to move on. And so, before I had a chance to ask you how you felt, or what was next, you asked me, "Why sausage?"

"You don't like sausage?" I asked.

"No," you said, taking a bite of the pizza and speaking now with your mouth full, "I was just wondering."

"Well," I said. "Me and some of the other guys in the department back home, we go to Uno's a lot, and we order the Chicago classic, which—"

"Has sausage on it," you said, cutting me off. "I get it."

"So," I said, "I figured I might as well see how the real thing compares."

"And?" you asked.

"It's good," I said. "Hearty."

You smiled, kept eating.

On the way back to the hotel, we passed by a store that was selling the latest version of your ex-husband's gadget. You paused there and said to me. "I appreciate you not asking me about it. I appreciate you not digging."

"You're welcome," I said, responding to the thank you that was said but not spoken.

We shared a cab out to O'Hare a couple of days later for our flights back home. You laid your head on my shoulder again, for the first time since New Orleans, and I think you fell asleep for a spell, but I didn't look. I closed my own eyes instead, and breathed in the scent of your hair—lavender and jasmine—remembering the conversation we'd had in the Crescent City.

"I doubt my wife would approve."

"My husband would shit himself."

Only one of them remained an obstacle, I thought to myself, before pushing the thought aside. An obstacle to what, I wondered. An obstacle to what?

🌸

PHILADELPHIA WAS BEDLAM. Or, well, the most memorable night of it was.

It was pouring rain and the two of us were out in it, trying to find a town car in which sat our keynote speaker for the evening, down from New York just for the occasion and trapped inside that vehicle with a driver who refused to take directions.

You were on your cell, trying to calm the poor woman, trying to, through her, convince the driver to just pull over. "A moving target," you said into your phone, "is only going to make this more difficult."

I checked my watch. We were already half an hour behind schedule. I asked you if you wanted me to head back inside and say something to the crowd.

You said, "I want you to keep looking for the car." So that's what I did.

It was a few minutes later that, patrolling the corner of Dock and 2nd Streets, I spotted the car a block north, driving west along Walnut. I screamed, "STOP!" at the top of my voice and the driver seemed to have heard me, even at that distance, for stop he did. You ran to me as I pointed.

"Look," I said, as one of the rear doors of the town car opened.

"I could kiss you," you told me. "And, in fact," you said, grabbing hold of my face in both your hands. "Why not?"

You pulled me in and laid one on me, a kiss that was trying so hard to be chaste that the effort involved erased any chance it had at innocence. You pulled back, held my left hand in both of yours, and fiddled with my wedding band. You stared at it for a moment but then, down the street, a door slammed, and that noise broke you from your reverie.

"Gotta go," you said, looking up at me.

And then you were gone.

It was in Denver that we said goodbye, a three-day-long goodbye that began with Hawaiian fish flown in that day to the most expensive seafood place you could find; that continued with a drunken evening of spoken word poetry in front of a pop art mural of a pair of puckered red lips; and that ended, with more drinking, in front of the hotel's piano at two in the morning the day that you handed in your resignation.

You played the opening riff to a song we had both known in college, and you sang, "Closing time. One last call for alcohol, so finish your whiskey or beer."

Then you pointed at me and I followed up, "Closing time. You don't have to go home, but you can't stay here."

We laughed, collected ourselves, then gulped down the seventh and eighth of the ten pancake shots the bartender had laid out for us.

"He had a crush on you," I told you. "No way he would have laid out this much otherwise."

You threw back the orange juice chaser. "It really does taste like pancakes," you said, licking your lips. "How does that work? I mean, seriously: how does that work?"

"I know not," I said. "I know not."

Out of nowhere—or at least it seemed like it came out of nowhere—you grabbed my leg and squeezed. "Have I told you?"

"Told me what?"

"I've met someone."

"You have?"

You bit down on your lower lip, tucking it underneath teeth tinted yellow by all the orange juice we'd been drinking, and you nodded, blushing.

"Me too," I said.

Your eyes widened and you looked down at my left hand, checking to see if the ring was still there. "You have? But wait," you said. "What about... what about—"

"Only a matter of time," I said. "She hasn't been happy in years. Nor I."

"Who?" you asked.

"A student," I said. "A former student, that is."

"For real?" you asked.

"Yes," I said, though every word of this was a lie.

"Wow," you said. "I'm glad. I was worried that... well, given what happened in Philadelphia last year. I..."

I ran a consoling hand along your shoulder. "I'm a big boy," I said.

"How big?" you joked. "After all, I've only just met the other guy."

We roared with laughter, falling into each other, into a hug that told the truth that I could not tell.

After a few moments, you pulled away and looked at me. You looked and you waited. And when still I said nothing, you tucked your bottom lip up under your teeth again and squinted at me. Then you grabbed the ninth of the shots that had been laid out for us and handed me the tenth and final one. We threw them back, then the chasers, and it was as you were wiping your mouth with the back of your sleeve that you asked me if I remembered *Top Gun*.

I nodded as you stood, as I looked up at you and tried to puzzle out what you were playing at.

You ran your fingers through my hair and I melted into you, closing my eyes as I rest my head against your stomach. You asked me, "Do you remember what Meg Ryan says to Goose? When they're in the bar?"

I couldn't. I shook my head no, the wool of your skirt scratching against my nose as I did.

It was as you slipped a hand down my neck and underneath my loosened collar that you said it. "Take me to bed," you said. "Or lose me forever."

I waited for you to laugh, to feel against my face the ripples of you busting a gut. But you didn't.

I remember fumbling up the escalator behind you, sweaty hand wrapped around sweaty hand. I remember looking down at the moving stairs to keep from looking at you, and then catching myself staring at your skirt instead, staring and thinking the drunken and/or juvenile thought that the view would be so much better from a couple steps further back. I remember punching myself in the thigh with my free hand, just for thinking that thought.

But I don't remember much after that. I think we opened your mini-bar for a bit more courage, but I'm not sure. All I do know is that I woke up in your arms the next day, that our shoes and socks and bottoms littered the floor around the bed, but that our shirts and underwear were still on.

"Did we?" I asked you as I sat up and rubbed at my temples.

You shrugged and smiled. "Does it matter?" you asked, and you patted a hand on my pillow, willing me to come back. When that didn't work, you held out your arms to me and gave me your best puppy dog eyes.

But I couldn't, and I told you as much as I dressed. I just couldn't.

❦

I'm STILL WITH JENNA, and you must know it; all it would take to know it is a glance at my status on this web that connects us ever so slightly, ever so completely. Things are better. We're getting there.

But I can't stop thinking, as I look at the photo of you and your swollen belly that ornaments your own corner of the web. I can't stop wondering if maybe it does matter what we did that night, if maybe it matters more than any other thing I've ever done in this world.

It wasn't supposed to happen. The doctors told me and Jenna as much. Told us again and again. But what if it did, Carrie? What if it did?

I can't stop wondering.

Yours,

Michael

Tracy folded the pages of the letter in half, then ran a finger along the crease, waiting for Michael to do something, to say something. But he didn't move. Though the rest of the scene had disappeared, he was still sitting up in bed, eyes on his laptop, its glowing screen all that illuminated his weary face. It was a long time before he said anything, but for the first time since they'd begun Tracy had no urge to fill the silence. She would wait, and wait she did.

He closed his laptop, the glowing apple on its backside blinking out as he did. Then he stepped out of bed and trudged back toward the defendant's platform, where the light shone down from above once more.

"So that's it?" he said, holding a hand to his stomach as if he'd been punched in the gut. "That's what all of this is about."

It was the beginning of it, she told him, but not all of it. "Mr. Silver," she said. "Do you recall where you were on the Tuesday evening before Thanksgiving this past year?"

"That was the night before your college visit," he said. "Right? When you came out to see the Manoa campus?"

"It was the night I arrived," said Tracy. "I flew in early."

"No, you didn't," said Michael. "We picked you up at the airport the next day."

"I came early," said Tracy, "to surprise you. But I was the one who was surprised."

"Waitaminute," said Michael. "When did you come? What did you see?"

Tracy banged her gavel down one last time, the judge's bench melting away as she did. The guards, too. She was on Michael's level now, where, she now realized, she should have been all along. The theatrics, the long and winding road to get here—they had been all for naught. He had scored just as many points as she had, maybe more. What mattered, all that mattered, was this: the confrontation. It was good that it would happen at the scene of the crime, rather than in any old room, but that was about all the magic was good for.

Hawaii was back, but not Michael's paradise. Not anymore.

Tracy stood in the shadows at the edge of Michael and Jenna's lanai, seeing but unseen. A real trick, that. But high atop the hill, with so much ocean to look at on two of the veranda's three open sides, wasn't it understandable that they might spend the least amount of time examining the side by the trees? If Tracy's mother had been with her, there might have been cause to look over here; they might all have been focused upon Veronica at the piano, the palms swaying in the breeze behind her as she made a requiem out of some piece of Top 40 schlock. But Veronica was not here. Tracy was alone, a backpack slung over shoulders slick with sweat from the climb, her suitcase leaned up against the side of the house. And before she could jump out from the trees to make them jump from their skins, she was stopped dead in her tracks by twin tableaux that made her own skin crawl.

Jenna was sitting on the chaise longue, her head hung low, a letter and an envelope clutched between trembling hands. Another woman, a lithe figure Tracy took to be one of Jenna's dancers, had her muscled arm around Jenna and was running a consoling hand up and down Jenna's shoulder.

Just a few feet from them, though it might as well have been at the other edge of the deep green sea, Michael was seated opposite a third woman. The two of them sat in wicker arm chairs and looked deep into each other's eyes as the woman held a baby in her outstretched arms, waiting. Waiting, it seemed, for Michael to take hold of the child himself.

This, Tracy would discover only later, was Carrie. And the child—the way that Michael looked at the child as he took it into his arms, his smiling face stained by tears; the way Carrie's concerned countenance twitched between Michael and Jenna, Jenna and Michael—Tracy decided that it had to be his. It wasn't possible—everyone knew he couldn't have kids—but here it was.

Tracy sank back further into the shadows, steadying herself on her suitcase and praying that none of them had seen her there. She closed her eyes, thought of the Michael she knew instead of the one before her now. Michael hadn't started things with Jenna until long after it would have been clear to anyone else that his relationship with Robin was over—it wasn't fucking, she finally admitted to herself; it was indeed making love. And then later, despite what happened, when the press dubbed Robin "Boston's most notorious rock and roll slut," Michael was the first person there to defend her and to call them out on their bullshit. When Veronica was pregnant with Tracy, and he wasn't even 15 yet, Michael was the one who stood up at Easter dinner and said it should be Vern's choice about the baby and not her father's.

Michael was a legend to Tracy, the perfect father figure for a girl who already had two awesome parents in the form of her moms. He was the cool rock and roll dad, but without all the bullshit baggage. He answered every email you sent him with an ass-kicking anecdote, he swooped in twice a year from 5,000 miles away with a new portrait of you gussied up as the bad-ass heroine du jour, and he was there when you and your moms needed him but got the hell out of the way when you didn't. When her mothers told her that Michael and Jenna weren't going to have kids, she cried because of how unfair it was that nobody would ever get to call him Daddy.

And yet—she opened her eyes again—here he was. Here he fucking was.

Tracy looked at Jenna again and began to cry for her now. Tracy knew how Jenna doted on her nieces and nephews up in Maine. She'd seen photos and videos of Jenna dancing with the tiny little girls and boys who took her creative movement classes back home in Hawaii, a line of smiling children bedecked in grass hula skirts and nearly fluorescent leis, each of them swaying their hips slightly out of time with the kid next to them. Jenna would never have any of that, thanks to the man she married. But now *he* had it! Now there was a baby falling to sleep on Michael's shoulder as he ran his fingers through its mop of brown hair.

That was enough for Tracy. She ran into the woods, down the hill, and out to the main road. She grabbed a taxi back to the airport, slept on a bench there, and waited to put on the show that she knew she must, the performance she'd been giving ever since.

"And that's all you saw?" said Michael, once they were back in the courtroom.

"Did I need to see more?" said Tracy.

"Yes!" yelled Michael. "See, the trouble is that, so far, you've only seen what you wanted to see. Let me show you—"

"What I wanted to see?!?" she shouted. "I didn't *want* to see any of it."

Michael stepped off of the accused's stand and, with a swift kick, sent it crashing into the darkness. "If it pleases the court," he said, "I'd like to submit a scene from the spring of 2010. It had been a month since I composed the email referenced by the prosecution, and several months before the scene we've just been made to watch. I was hosting the bachelor party for a colleague from the university."

As he continued speaking, the scene formed around him. He was in a hotel room, a half-dozen easels standing between him and a naked woman sprawled out on a couch. It was Jenna's dancer friend, Tracy realized after a moment of gawking, the one who had been consoling her. Tracy scoffed, wondering how this scene would help prove his innocence. Then Michael's clothes disappeared, save his boxers.

"Christ," she mumbled. What the fuck was this meant to prove?

"It was only once we were alone together that I began to sweat," he said. "Half the guys had left by midnight, thanking me for the invitation and for the entertainment. The groom-to-be had left for the next room, led off by the bustier of the two performers. And the last guy, a gay poet whose motives for coming had been unclear all night—once he'd finished counting out the five hundred-dollar bills he had agreed to leave for the groom's seductress, he stepped out into the yard with a couple of cold ones to chat it up with the security guy, who, it turned out, was gay too.

"That left Amber and me—"

Tracy scoffed again. The stripper's name was fucking Amber? Of course it was.

Michael ignored her and continued. "That left Amber and me, and now she was asking—"

"Where do you want me?" said Amber.

Michael scanned the room, then pointed. "Over there, on the floor, against that bare wall. And you'll need..." He looked around again. "Your stockings. Your stockings and shoes."

She pushed herself off of the couch, then navigated her way through the maze of easels toward where he'd directed her.

For the first time, Michael seemed to notice his own near

nakedness. "Shit," he said, "you don't mind that I'm down to my—"

"All's fair in love and Strip Pictionary," she said.

"I know," he said, "I know. But I did take off my shirt of my own free will after the beer-induced hot flashes began. I can put everything back on, if it'd make you feel more comfortable."

She shook her head, chuckling. "This has to be the strangest party I've ever done."

Michael searched the room for a clean canvas as she pulled on the first of her stockings. "Only one should be all the way on," he said, not even looking at her. "The right one. The pose will be you pulling on the left one."

"Got it," she said.

He set the last blank canvas on the easel he'd been using all night.

"Do Isis and I get to keep any of these?" she asked as she sat down.

"To be honest," he said, "most of them are crap."

"Not yours," she said.

"Even mine aren't all that—"

"You're too damned modest," she said.

Michael blushed. "Okay," he said, getting back to business. "Lean back against the wall. Keep your right leg flat on the floor, and lift your left leg up."

She nodded, then did just as she was told.

"Right," he said, "that's great. Keep your knee at about the same level as your chin—yes, bring the chin down if you need to—and keep your eyes focused on the stocking as you're pulling it down."

"How far down?" she asked.

"About mid-calf," he said. "And make sure you're using both hands to pull it down. But gently," he added. "Slowly, I mean. You're not in a rush."

She smiled. "You needn't be in a rush, either, Mr. Silver. I can't leave until Isis is done in the other room. We've got plenty of time."

"I don't know about that," he said. "This is only my friend's second or third time. He's only a PhD candidate, after all. They were probably done before she got his pants down."

Amber chuckled.

"Sorry if I seem frazzled," he said. "I just want to get this one right."

"You apologize too much, too," she said. "Your wife the cause of that?"

"No," he said. "That'd probably be my sister."

"Your sister, the stripper?"

"That's the one," he said, beginning to sketch the line of Amber's arched back. "She's been making me feel like I have something to apologize for since the day my parents brought her home from the hospital."

"And she's the reason that this evening was about easels instead of dildos, right?"

Michael nodded. "The others had him convinced about the traditional bachelor party, but I've never been one to keep things traditional. And, I mean, when your sister's in the profession..."

Amber said, "She the reason you're so afraid of looking at me?"

Michael stopped sketching. "What do you mean?" he said.

"You haven't looked at me all night," said Amber. "Not really. At least not since I took my clothes off. The sketches you've done have been great, but they've all been from memory. Haven't they?"

Tracy watched the lump form in Michael's throat, watching him swallow it back. He was caught. Guilty. Again, Tracy wondered why he was showing her this scene, what it was meant to accomplish. A stripper calling him on his subterfuge? This was meant to make him look *less* guilty?

"This one's a Nick Gold," he said. "From an old trading card set of her best pin-ups."

"Her?" said Amber. "Isn't Nick a man's name?"

Michael put down his pencil—in order, it seemed, to pontifi-cate. "It was a pseudonym," he said. "Nick was actually a woman by the name of—"

"Pick up the pencil," said Amber. "Isn't that the rule, that you never take your pencil up off the page?"

In spite of herself, Tracy was beginning to like this one. She'd comforted Jenna at a critical moment, or, well, she was going to eventually, and she was giving Michael shit when shit was what he deserved—why should Tracy let Michael's infatuation with this woman influence her opinion of her?

Michael began to sketch again. "How did you know?" he asked. "How did you know I was doing it from memory?"

"I saw how nervous you were when one of your buddies picked a pose early on, when he set up something you had never seen before."

Michael snickered. "I don't think that pose had been seen by anyone on Earth before."

"It was pretty hard to hold," said Amber.

Michael smiled, lightening up. His hand flowed across the canvas now, no longer skittish and uncertain. He captured the arc of her back, the slight roll of flesh at her midsection, the way one breast drooped just a smidgen more than the other. He seemed the least certain of his work on her feet; an old insecurity, Tracy happened to know.

"Can I be honest?" he asked her.

"Absolutely," said Amber. "Lay it on me. I did take one semester of psych at U of H before dropping out."

"It's all about something my sister said to me once. Or, well, something she said about me."

"And that was?"

Michael worked fast now, as if the conversation had drowned out the nagging voice of his inner critic. He said nothing for a moment as he captured her pouty lips, the severe line of her bangs. Then he said, "My sister once told me I'd never been able to say no to a pretty girl in my life."

"Wow," said Amber. "Harsh much?"

"Sure, but it's also true," said Michael, sketching now the parts of her he might have been embarrassed to approach earlier: her nipples, her narrow strip of pubic hair. "And it makes me worry," he said."

"Looking at another girl isn't a crime," she said. "Neither is thinking about one."

"But acting on those thoughts," said Michael, "acting on those thoughts *is* a crime. The worst crime. Isn't it?"

Amber broke her pose and turned toward him, but it didn't matter now. He was almost done.

"Have you ever done that?" she asked him. "Do you have any real reason to be worried?"

"Kinda," said Michael. "Yes."

"You've cheated on your wife?" said Amber.

"I cheated *with* my wife, back in the day. Or, well, the other relationship was pretty much over. So—"

"OK," said Amber, "so that doesn't count."

"But there was this woman that I met while attending conferences over the last couple of years..."

As he trailed off, Tracy leaned forward in her seat. This was it. Was he going to admit to this stranger what he couldn't tell her. What he *wouldn't* tell her?

"We had this one night," said Michael.

"And what?" said Amber. "You fooled around a little? She sucked your dick?"

"I don't know," said Michael. "We had a lot to drink."

"Well," said Amber. "That doesn't count. Or, well, you can't be sure. So what the hell, right? Give yourself a break!"

"But I wanted it to happen," said Michael. "I wanted it to happen so Goddamned much."

"And have you ever felt that way before?" said Amber. "About anyone else."

"I feel that way right now," said Michael.

"Oh," said Amber, smiling.

"But I don't want you to," said Michael, putting his hands up in front of him. "I want you to ignore that, to resist——"

"I don't know," said Amber, staying put, heeding him in action if not in speech. "You're looking mighty cute in your underwear there, Mr. Silver."

"You mean you would?" said Michael. "If I wanted to, right now, then you——"

"Of course I would," said Amber. "But you don't want to."

"But I do," said Michael.

"If you wanted to," said Amber, "you'd be over here right now."

Michael wove his way through the easels to her. And, as he did, she stood to receive him. They moved ever so close to each other, ever so close, but still far enough away that he could feign innocence if they were caught. Then they drew closer. His hands hovered over her hips; hers reached for his ass. Their fingers curled in anticipation, the two of them ready to puncture that final invisible barrier. He pressed his face close to hers, their eyes closing, their mouths opening. Tracy caught sight of the head of his penis, that awful, deceitful creature rising from its slumber, seeking out the fertile ground it could smell, could almost taste.

Then, at the last minute, Michael pulled away. He shoved his dick back into the folds of his boxers and stalked back across the room. "I am such an asshole," he said. "I love my wife, but——"

"Does she know about these moments?" said Amber.

"Every single one," said Michael. "I haven't been able to keep a secret from that woman since the day I met her."

Tracy found this hard to believe. Did Jenna know about the email yet? Would he tell her about this night, the one he was showing Tracy right now, or would it be Amber who did that?

How could Jenna know all of this and still hold his hand? How could she know this and still laugh at his jokes—his *terrible* jokes?

"So, she knows," said Amber. "Key question then is, is she OK with it?"

"She says she's fine with it," said Michael. "She says she understands. But how can she? Does she really understand how close I've come?"

"Close only counts in horseshoes and hand grenades," said Amber.

"What if I *am* a grenade?" said Michael. "What happens when I go off?"

Amber crossed to him and grabbed ahold of his crotch. She pulled him close, pressing her breasts against his naked chest, rubbing a thigh against him, pulling his package toward her own groin. It was an invitation she was waiting to see if he'd RSVP to. But he gave no response, neither accepting nor declining.

Instead, he blurted out "I'm worried I got her pregnant."

Amber let him go and laughed. "Who?" she said. "Your wife?"

"No," he said. "The other woman. Carrie."

Amber nodded. Then she held up a finger and crossed to the door that led to the other room. She held an ear to the door for a few moments, smirked, then nodded again.

"There are tests," she said, as she collected her clothes from the floor.

Michael, taking her cue, began to get dressed himself.

"Have you asked her to get the baby tested?" she asked. "I think it's pretty simple. You swab the inside of your cheek, she swabs the inside of the baby's, and you send the swabs off to a lab."

"I wrote her an email," he said as he zipped up his jeans. "But I never sent it."

With her hands behind her back to fasten her bra, Amber couldn't throw anything at him, but it looked like she wanted to. Instead, she rolled her eyes and sighed.

"How do you even broach that subject?" said Michael.

"Is the other guy still around?" asked Amber as she stepped back into her dress. "Or other guys, plural?"

"Only one," said Michael as he pulled his shirt back on. "And no," he said. "That dude split the moment she told him she was pregnant."

"Mind giving me a hand?" she asked him, nodding over her shoulder at the zipper to her dress.

He had a bit of trouble with it and he asked, "How did Isis do this with her teeth?"

"Girl's got skills," she said. "Anyway," she said, turning around to face him, "way I see it is that you want to let this woman, this—"

"Carrie," he said.

"Carrie," she said. "You want to let Carrie know that you're not like the other dude, right? That you're *not* going to duck your responsibilities."

"Right," he said.

"And your wife already knows?" she said. "She knows all of it?"

Michael nodded. Tracy couldn't believe it, but Michael nodded.

"Then it's settled," she said, pulling a phone from her purse and swiping its screen to unlock it. "Give me their numbers. I'm going to make shit happen."

"You?" he said with a snicker. "I didn't see 'making shit happen' on your menu. What's it going to cost me?"

She shook her phone at him. "Phone numbers," she said. "And no more stalling. Like your sister said, you can't say no to a pretty girl."

He took her phone and tapped away at it for a minute. Then he handed it back to her. She stuffed it back into her purse as the door to the other room began to creak open.

"Why would you do this for me?" he asked, slipping his coat back on. "We just met."

"*Almost Famous*," she said. "Or *Elizabethtown*. Or any Cameron Crowe movie you'd like, really. See," she said, smiling as she straightened the lapels of his jacket, "I've been one cliché for most of my life. I've always wondered what it would feel like to be a different one."

He smirked. "The manic pixie dream girl," he said. "You do look a little like Kirsten Dunst."

"All I need is a beret," she said. "Right? And then the picture's complete."

"And a quirky saying," he said with a laugh. "You need a quirky saying."

"It's all happening," she said, kissing him on the cheek as Isis emerged from the other room. Then the scene faded away and Michael and Tracy were back in the courtroom, the jury abuzz with hushed conversation, a hundred redheads whispering into each other's ears about good old Michael Silver. His dream come true.

"She made good on her promise," said Michael, still lost in the memory and not looking at Tracy. "She made shit happen. On the Tuesday evening before Thanksgiving, this past year—"

"Waitaminute," said Tracy. "You mean to tell me—"

"Oh yeah," said Michael, turning finally to face her. "The same night you thought I ruined my marriage for good was the night that Amber helped me make it all better. I was just coming back from my last class before the Thanksgiving break. And when I walked onto my porch, what did I see?"

He snapped his fingers and they were back on the lanai. But this time it was earlier, and it was his story, and the sound was on.

When Michael walked in, Jenna was just finishing the tale of a camping trip she and Michael had taken some ten years before with her dance company back home. The girls in the company had left clumps of sodden toilet paper and spilled dog food behind for Michael, the conscientious former Boy Scout, to clean up, and he had grumbled about it the whole time, wondering aloud if the toilet paper was wet because of the rain or because of what it had been used to wipe, but somehow over the course of that chore, or during the drive home afterward, he had convinced himself to ask Jenna to marry him.

"And he says to me," said Jenna, "'I hope this isn't considered some form of infidelity, me touching the TP they used to wipe their pee-pees and all.'"

Amber and Carrie laughed and laughed, spilling wine in the process, as Michael, pale as a ghost, said, trying to make a joke, "Honey, I'm home."

The three women turned to face him, silencing their laughter. Jenna finished off her glass of wine, then stood up, wrapped her arms around him, and planted a big kiss on his cheek.

"Hello, dear," she said. "Surprise!"

Amber stood to hug him next. And, as she did, she told him that she and Jenna had picked Carrie and the baby up at the airport that afternoon.

"The baby," Michael mumbled as Jenna stepped aside to let Amber hug him.

"Logan," said Carrie, who stood now too, and who nodded at a cloth play mat that had been laid upon the floor.

As Amber drew back and Carrie waited her turn to greet him, Michael looked down upon the sleeping boy who might be his son. It was a different look than the one Tracy had seen, not yet that mash-up of sadness and joy that would be playing upon his face when she snuck through the trees in just a few minutes. It was a look of pure wonder.

"He's beautiful," he said.

"Thank you," said Carrie as they hugged, as they held each other for the first time in over a year. Tracy watched them, waiting for some sign of... of what she wasn't sure. But some sign of something.

"We have the results," said Jenna as Michael and Carrie parted. She held up the still sealed envelope, a nervous smile on her face.

"You got any more wine?" he asked.

Jenna poured them each a glass and they took up their positions in the tableaux that Tracy was about to walk in on. Jenna and Amber sat off to the side, giving space to the other two. Michael held the envelope in his hands, but they were shaking so hard that Tracy didn't see any way he could open it himself.

And that's when he, weakling that he was, asked his wife to do it for him.

"I wasn't weak," he said aloud, addressing Tracy as if he had heard her thoughts. "She had asked me if she could open it when it came. It was as much her right as it was mine."

But Tracy didn't care. She didn't want to hear any more. She just wanted to see. She wanted to see it happen, the moment she had missed.

Jenna slipped a finger under the sealed flap of the envelope and tore it open. Slowly, she removed the single sheet of paper that was inside. And even more slowly, she unfolded it. She read silently for a moment, and then the first tear slipped out of the corner of her eye.

"He's not yours," she told her husband.

Tracy gasped. She felt her body quiver at the sound of the words. Her arms began to tremble first, then her legs, and then something deep in her chest—her heart, she supposed—began to shudder from the effort to keep her upright and conscious. She doubled over just as Jenna bent forward, just as Amber wrapped her arm around her.

Then the baby let out a soft cry. He was awake and his mother was picking him up.

"Would you like to hold him?" Carrie asked Michael.

"But he's not," Michael began, then trailed off.

"Does it matter?" asked Carrie, holding the baby out for him to take.

Tracy looked up and caught sight of herself creeping through the trees. She studied the look on her face, the anger there, the incredible sadness. Then she watched herself disappear.

"I held him for a few minutes," Michael told her now, as the scene began to fast-forward before them, "before he fell asleep again on my shoulder. Then I brought him to the other room, to the pack-and-play crib Carrie had brought with her. When I came back, the girls were drinking again, trading more stories about me, and they had come up with an idea."

Michael returned to the scene and stepped into the room. The women looked back at him with conspiratorial smirks upon their faces.

"What?" he said, taking a seat and running his fingers through his now-disheveled hair.

"I've had an idea," said Carrie. "Something we're going to do to turn this night around and turn that frown upside down."

"Please don't tell me we're going for the *Chasing Amy*," said Michael. "Because, as hot as that scenario was in my mind's eye like thirteen years ago, the realities of it, now that it's right in front of me, are too Goddamned weird."

"Nope," said Jenna. "We're going to recreate a painting."

And Tracy knew just which one they were talking about. There was a Nick Gold pin-up called "The Temptresses," one of Michael's favorites—the one he'd referred to the most in his thesis, as it happened—and it involved three naked women surrounding a dapper young man in a suit. There was a blonde, a brunette, and a redhead, just as there were here and now, and they each draped themselves over or wrapped themselves around a different part of the dude, trying to draw his attention away from the painter, the viewer, who he had locked his eyes on.

"And you're okay with this?" Michael asked Jenna. "Me, surrounded by three naked women?"

"We're not the ones who are going to be naked," said Amber.

"Wait," said Michael, fidgeting in his seat, "what?"

"It's a reversal," said Carrie.

"So get up," said Jenna, gulping down the last of her wine. "And get naked."

"Uh-uh," said Michael. "No way."

Amber laughed, reminded Michael that he was outnumbered, and then gave him some speech about how torturing himself wasn't doing him any good, wasn't doing his marriage any good. She intimated that maybe them torturing him instead would be a bigger help.

Michael folded his arms across his chest, defiant.

"Who do you think is going to do this more gently," said Carrie, "you, or us?"

He shook his head.

And that was Jenna pulled him to his feet. As she did, Amber raced over and tugged at his shirt, untucking it, trying to get it off of him. But then he skittered away, putting the table between them. Then they chased each other, taunting and teasing each other as they ran.

"You've probably jerked off to this very idea at least a half dozen times," Carrie told him.

"Only once," he said.

Jenna caught her husband and got his shirt up over his head. He blushed and looked down at the floor. Amber poured him a glass of wine—quite sloppily, Tracy noted—and handed it to him.

"Is this really going to solve anything?" he asked, in between gulps from the glass.

Jenna lifted his chin up before he could have himself a good and proper sulk. "It will if you let it," she said.

Michael took a moment to think, then nodded, convinced. Amber yanked his pants to the floor and he stepped out of them, clad now only in a pair of SpongeBob SquarePants boxers emblazoned with the words "It's a Yellow Thang!" Amber laughed at them.

"My niece bought them for me as a joke one year," he said. "Though she was little, and probably didn't get it, and it was probably her mothers' idea."

Jenna latched her fingers onto the waistband of Michael's underwear now, as if to pull it down. "You ready?" she asked him.

"Who's going to paint it, anyway?" said Michael, stalling.

"You, silly," said Amber. "We'll shoot reference photos, and you can get started as soon as we're done."

"I don't have to do it tonight," said Michael, trying, as always, to get out of anything uncomfortable.

"Oh yeah, you do," said Jenna. "That's part of the plan. Operation Catharsis. We're going to stay right here and watch you do it."

"This is ridiculous," said Michael.

"No," said Carrie. "Living the way you live, like guilt is some cologne you put on, or a body wash you scrub into your pores every day—that's ridiculous."

Jenna's fingers were still latched onto Michael's underwear, ready to do the deed, a deed she'd probably done hundreds of times before, but never, Tracy thought, in front of a third party, let alone a fourth.

"Jenna," said Michael, "I—"

Jenna took his face into her hands. "What?" she said.

"Can't I just paint in the naughty bits later?" he asked.

"Do you really think that would have the same effect?" said Jenna.

"I know what my dick looks like," said Michael.

"Yeah," said Carrie, setting up the camera now, "but we don't!"

Michael and Jenna stared at each other for a moment, until Michael blinked and looked down.

"I promise," he said. "I promise—"

"I know," she said, giving him a kiss. "I wish you wouldn't."

Tracy cried at this, at Jenna's generosity, her understanding. How could she forgive him, not only for the betrayals gone by but for all those yet to come? Tracy could never do that, *would* never. She wiped at her eyes with the sleeve of her judge's robe. Was Jenna the better woman, or the worse?

Jenna stepped away from Michael, then looked over at Carrie. "Where do you want us?"

She waved them into position, giving them instructions. Michael stood center. Amber stood to his right, back arched against his side, hand on his thigh. Jenna went behind him, arm coming up over his left shoulder, face pressed against his right cheek. And Carrie, once she'd finished setting the camera, she grabbed a remote and went to Michael's left side, mirroring Amber.

Amber said, "You ready, Michael?"

"As I'll ever be," he said.

Carrie snapped the photo and the world went white for a

second, then black. Tracy closed her eyes, opened them. The flash went off again, capturing not the women but the mannequins, not the house in Hawaii but the theater on Cape Cod. Michael was slumping to the floor. Tracy looked around herself. Her judge's robes were gone, her podium. She was back in the lighting booth, looking down at her uncle, who lay on the floor, shuddering, as naked as he had been in the dream, his clothes scattered across the stage. Something flashed before her eyes a third time, perhaps the last of the drugs leaving her mind. She rushed to the stage.

He was shaking, Michael, mumbling something she couldn't make out at first.

"Michael?" she said, kneeling down to touch him, to search his wrist for a pulse.

"Not guilty," he said. "I'm not guilty."

"I know," she said, though she was anything but certain of that fact. She felt his forehead to see what his temperature might be, pushing sweaty, matted hair out of her way.

"Tell me I'm not guilty," said Michael, his shaking calming to a steady shiver.

Despite the fact that she wasn't sure, that she hadn't decided yet, Tracy pronounced him not guilty. *Not innocent either*, she thought, but did not say.

"Good," he said. "Now, go to hell."

He shook once more, a violent shake that ended with his eyes closed and his breathing shallow. Tracy stepped away from him, back into the darkness. She looked at him, sleeping in his pool of light, and then she ran. She ran to the house. She ran to the women who slept there. They would know what to do. They had to.

The police were not involved, nor the hospital. Michael was brought to the house, to the bed he shared with his wife, and she kept watch over him. Desiree and Veronica sent Tracy to bed, told her she'd be spoken to in the morning. And so, Tracy had gone to her room and done as she was told. But she couldn't sleep. And the moment that the sun began to rise over Nantucket Sound, a moment in their family that was understood to be the earliest one should ever rise, she snuck out the back door and made her way to the barn, to the theater.

She dressed in her stage blacks, though it was hours before the call for that day's matinée, and she pulled her hair back into a severe ponytail, yanking a stray hair out of her scalp when it dared to fly loose.

Once the chair and the table were set, she sat and worked at stuffing the bloodied and muddied boot into the box from which it was meant to be withdrawn. It was a tight squeeze, the box not built for the task—it was a holdover from a production of *Alice in Wonderland*, in fact, meant to be used for the largest size cake and nothing more.

The front door creaked open out in the hallway, but she didn't look up, didn't want to know. This was going to be bad, whoever it was.

"How you feeling?" asked Veronica.

"Sore," said Tracy, trying one last time to shove the damned boot into the box.

"Sore how?" said Veronica. "Emotionally sore?"

"No," said Tracy, giving up, slamming the lid of the box down upon the twisted leather of the boot, half of it still hanging loose. "I'm sore sore," she said. "I can barely walk straight."

"Wait," said Veronica. "Why—"

Tracy looked over her shoulder to see the look on her mother's face, to see if she was trying to pull one over on her, but Veronica looked genuinely mystified.

Tracy said: "Don't tell me Desiree actually managed to keep the secret."

"Oh," said Veronica, "your date."

Veronica sat on the arm of the chair, looking off into the middle distance. She breathed in deep, let out a heavy sigh.

"Don't worry," said Tracy. "He didn't hurt me. Or, well... I'm hurting, but... Forget it."

"Forgotten," said Veronica, squeezing Tracy's shoulder. "Too much information, anyway. I assume you were safe about it. And that you know it doesn't *have* to hurt. Not always."

"Of course," said Tracy.

"Do you want to be even safer?" said Veronica. "I mean, we can go to the doctor, get a prescription."

"I've already set up an appointment," said Tracy. "For Monday."

Veronica looked down at her, looked her right in the eye, and stared. She seemed to see something in Tracy that Tracy couldn't see herself. Veronica didn't seem to want to look away. She didn't blink, she didn't flinch; she just stared. And, after a minute, it was too much. So, Tracy looked away. She looked away, fiddled with the boot again—which cooperated this time—and then stood.

"Did Michael and Jenna leave?" said Tracy, walking away.

"They're packing the car now," said Veronica. "They're headed up to Maine to visit her family before their flight back to Honolulu."

"Did he say anything?" said Tracy, plucking props from her milk crate and setting them.

"He said a lot of things," said Veronica.

"About what happened last night?"

"And the night of my own fucked-up dream, too."

Tracy turned to face her mother again. "I was little," she said. "I didn't know what I was—"

"I know," said Veronica, standing now, crossing to Tracy, "but you knew what you were doing last night."

"If you'd seen what I saw," said Tracy, "wouldn't you have wanted some answers?"

It was a dumb question to ask. Of course Veronica could understand the need for answers. She woke to the sound of her parents screaming at each other at least once a week when she was a kid, her own mother yelling at her father, "Why don't you run away then, if that'd make you happier?" And he'd yell back, "You wouldn't understand." But, try as they all did to understand, he never did give them answers.

"I should've stayed quiet?" said Tracy. "I should have let that image fester in my mind?"

Veronica said: "You could have just asked him."

"But," said Tracy, "look at the men in our family, Mum. What reason did I have to expect he'd tell me the truth?"

"Because Michael isn't like the rest of them," said Veronica. "You knew that before this all started and you know it now. Why you ever thought—"

"I thought it," said Tracy, "because they all let you down, eventually. Your father left—"

"Actually, my mother left him."

"My father left," said Tracy.

"He's not your father," said Veronica. "He never was."

"And, yeah," said Tracy, "maybe Michael has resisted every temptation, up until now. Maybe he didn't fuck Carrie. But maybe he did. And, even if he didn't, then someday, someday he might—"

Veronica shook her head. "Do you have a crystal ball I don't know about?"

"What?" said Tracy.

"Can you predict the future?" said Veronica, grabbing her daughter's arms, looking her in the eyes again in that way only mothers seemed capable of doing.

"Oh, give me a break," said Tracy, shrugging off her mother's hands, turning away. "I can make an educated guess, Mum, based on the evidence. And there's a whole lot of it."

"Whatever happened to 'innocent until proven guilty'?"

But she had already proven him guilty. Maybe not of the big crimes, but what about the fact that he'd fessed up to so many of the little ones? This wasn't the trial anymore. This was the parole hearing. This was about his likelihood to offend again. But Veronica couldn't see that.

"This is about something bigger than Michael," said Veronica. "In your mind, this is about whether or not any man is likely to offend, isn't it? Michael's just the scapegoat."

"Not a scapegoat," said Tracy. "A representative. He's the mean, the average. And if he can't be trusted..."

"He's one man," said Veronica. "Just like the Runt is one man. And my father, too."

"But together, they're a pattern," said Tracy. "Together—"

"Christ!" said Veronica. "Did we ever tell you that all men were evil? Or is this just what happens to the daughter of dykes, that you grow up thinking—"

"Not all men!" shouted Tracy. "I had this one hope, this one shining example. And now it's gone. Now he's gone! Off of the pedestal I put him on, his visage shattered on the cold, hard ground."

Veronica chuckled, then composed herself. "His visage?" she said.

How could she laugh, even for a moment? Yes, it had been an obnoxious choice of words—*Visage, Tracy? Really?*—but the truth was that Michael *was* a hero to her, as much a hero as Zeus was to the Olympians, or Helios to the Rhodians. But he was more in her world, not one of seven wonders, but *the* wonder, and he was never supposed to fall, not him.

"If you don't understand how much it hurts," said Tracy. "If you don't understand—"

Tracy broke down as her mother wrapped her arms around her, the tears flowing, the snot clogging her nose, sobs choking back the words she wanted to say, but could not.

"I do understand," said Veronica. "Fathers are never what you want them to be, not forever at least. None of them are perfect."

"But he was supposed to be," said Tracy, stuttering through her tears. "Goddamn it."

They held each other for a moment more, but Tracy soon pulled away and wiped at her face with the long sleeves of her stage blacks. Behind her, she heard Veronica pick up the teacup from the table, then a sploosh of something hitting the water within it.

"Here," said Veronica. "Have some tea."

Tracy turned around and gave her mother a weak smile. "It's not tea, Mum. It's just water."

Veronica showed her a small vial, rolled it between her forefinger and thumb. "I put some chamomile in it. I think that'll take the edge off, either way."

Tracy took the cup and sipped.

"Got anything stronger," she said. "I am 18, after all."

Veronica smirked. "You don't need anything stronger, Trace."

Tracy sat in the chair, sipped again.

"Am I in trouble?" said Tracy.

"I don't know," said Veronica. "You tell me."

They stared at each other for a moment before Tracy spoke again.

"Did you get what I was saying about the boot? My theory?"

"Sure," said Veronica. "It's a metaphor."

"Are you making fun of me?" said Tracy, setting the teacup down on its saucer. "I mean, I'm serious: doesn't it represent the life he wished he had?"

"It was just a boot," said Veronica, running her hand over the top of the box it was now hidden in. "It's what mariners wore."

"You don't think it meant anything?" said Tracy.

"The boot was all they had of him," said Veronica. "His wife hid it beneath the floorboards of the kitchen because she couldn't bear her children looking at the nightmare of it, but also because she couldn't bear to part with the only piece of him that she had left. It was only a piece, and it might have been the piece she detested the most, but it was him, the one she loved. So she kept it. Because it reminded her of all the other pieces, which, though they were lost to the world, belonged to her forever."

"Oh," said Tracy.

"Do you understand?" said Veronica.

She nodded.

"You going to chill out in here for a while?" said Veronica.

She nodded again.

"Okay," said Veronica. "Take a nap. You could use one."

Veronica bent down and rubbed her nose against Tracy's. Her forehead pressed against Tracy's as she gave her daughter's neck a quick squeeze and a rub. And then, Veronica was gone.

Tracy took one more sip of the tea, then set it down on the table. She opened the lid of the box, the boot popping free and landing with a thud on the table. She stared at it for a moment, and then, just as she had the night before, she took off her own shoe.

The boot slid on without a struggle; it fit. Well enough to walk in, she imagined, though she wasn't going to try. She was too sleepy.

"You had a small foot, old man," she said, yawning.

Tracy picked up the tea, leaned back into the cushions of the chair, and put her feet up on the table. She took a final sip, then set the now-empty cup upside down on her belly. She watched it rise and fall, rise and fall. Her eyes began to flicker closed, first on the rises, then on the falls as well. She felt the cup there, on her belly, for a moment more, felt a leftover drop seep through her shirt. But then that was gone, too. And she was somewhere else.

Tracy stood outside a courthouse now, looking up at a piano falling from the sky.

Beside her, someone said, "You might want to move."

It was a man in paint-stained jeans and a torn Voltron t-shirt. On his head, he wore an off-white hard hat emblazoned with a bell inside a circle. He smirked at her, rolling up a comic book and slipping it into his back pocket.

"Just a suggestion," he said.

And because she wondered what he might say next, because she wanted to know, she did move.

"What's with the helmet?" she asked him.

"Oh this?" he said, as he rapped a fist against it. "I fell in love with long distances." He smirked. Then, with a tilt of his head, a raise of his eyebrows, and just the slightest quaver in his voice, he added, "That is the line, isn't it?"

She laughed at his joke, his dumb reference—the best olive branch he had to offer—and she walked with him, happy to have some part of him back, the part that was true and always would be.

☙❦☙

The Silver Family's story continues in The Chains of Desire, *wherein we learn of the forbidden romance between two of Tracy's childhood heroes: her Aunt Ashley and the rock star Robin Gates.*

ACKNOWLEDGMENTS

A portion of this novel was originally performed as the stage play *The People vs. Jesus Christ*. This play premiered at Bradford College in Haverhill, Massachusetts in March 1999.

The cast of the production included Robert DaPonte as Michael, Jonathan Martin as Adam, Trish Ruppert as Jenna, Amanda Damstra as Maggie, Tori Ryan as Mary, and Chris Larsen as Andy the Chinese Food Delivery Boy. I directed. Nikki St. Pierre, Heather Thatcher, Lissa Brennan, and Matt Perrone were our crew.

❦

Other portions of this novel were originally performed as the stage play *Temptress*. This play premiered at the Players' Ring in Portsmouth, New Hampshire in January 2014.

The production was directed by Jonathan Martin and stage-managed by Michelle Blouin-Wright. Sean O'Connell designed the props.

The cast included me as Michael; Crystal Lisbon as Jenna; Liz Locke as Veronica; Meghan D. Morash as Tracy; Jennifer Henry as

Desiree and Carrie; Lizbeth Myers as Robin and Amber; Samantha Bagdon as Tana, Guard, and Student; Gwyn Codd as Tori, Guard, and Student; and Michael Lavoie as Tucker, The Runt, and George.

৩✹১

Special thanks to my undergraduate writing mentor David Crouse, and to my grad school mentors Michael Lowenthal, Christina Shea, Tony Eprile, and Rachel Kadish.

Crystal Lisbon, Mary Casiello, Jonathan Martin, R.T. Tompkins, and Jena Marie DiPinto read drafts of *Temptress* and offered invaluable feedback.

Mary, alongside Lissa Brennan and Chuck Galle, served as beta readers on the earliest prose version of this book.

Ali Russo and Viktor Herrmann served as my final beta readers.

Abbie Levesque copyedited. Any remaining errors are the result of my own stubbornness or stupidity. Abbie is the best.

ABOUT THE AUTHOR

E. Christopher Clark is the author of the Stains of Time series, a family saga with a hint of magical realism and a whole lot of time travel. His other books include the short story collections *Out of the Woods* and *Under the World*, the novella *The Seven Wives of Silver*, and a collection of poems cheekily titled *Bad Poetry Night*. His short stories have been published in *Live Free or Ride: Tales of the Concord Coach*, *River Muse: Tales of Lowell & the Merrimack Valley*, and the University of Hawaii's *Vice-Versa*. A graduate of Lesley University's MFA in Creative Writing program, he lives in Massachusetts with his wife and daughters.

echristopherclark.com

facebook.com/eccbooks

x.com/eccbooks

instagram.com/eccbooks

goodreads.com/eccbooks

pinterest.com/eccbooks

amazon.com/E.-Christopher-Clark/e/B00H0G94T0